Linda I
San Francisco where she is public information director for the Exploratorium, a science museum. She counsels other women with breast cancer. This is her first book.

Linda Dackman UP FRONT

Sex and the Post-Mastectomy Woman

PENGUIN BOOKS

PENGUIN BOOKS
Published by the Penguin Group
Viking Penguin, a division of Penguin Books USA Inc.,
375 Hudson Street, New York, New York 10014, U.S.A.
Penguin Books Ltd, 27 Wrights Lane, London W8 5TZ, England
Penguin Books Australia Ltd, Ringwood, Victoria, Australia
Penguin Books Canada Ltd, 2801 John Street,
Markham, Ontario, Canada L3R 1B4
Penguin Books (N.Z.) Ltd, 182–190 Wairau Road,
Auckland 10, New Zealand

Penguin Books Ltd, Registered Offices:
Harmondsworth, Middlesex, England

First published in the United States of America by
Viking Penguin, a division of Penguin Books USA Inc., 1990
Published in Penguin Books 1991

1 3 5 7 9 10 8 6 4 2

Copyright © Linda Dackman, 1990
All rights reserved

Portions of this book first appeared in different form
in *Vogue* as "Sex and the Single-Breasted Woman."

LIBRARY OF CONGRESS CATALOGING IN PUBLICATION DATA
Dackman, Linda.
Up front: sex and the post-mastectomy woman/Linda Dackman.
p. cm.
Reprint. Originally published: New York: Viking, 1990.
ISBN 0 14 01.1260 X
1. Mastectomy—Patients—Sexual behavior. 2. Mastectomy—
Psychological aspects. 3. Interpersonal relations. I. Title.
RD667.5.D33 1991
616.99′449059′019—dc20   90–21629

Printed in the United States of America

Except in the United States of America,
this book is sold subject to the condition
that it shall not, by way of trade or otherwise,
be lent, re-sold, hired out, or otherwise circulated
without the publisher's prior consent in any form of
binding or cover other than that in which it is
published and without a similar condition
including this condition being imposed
on the subsequent purchaser.

To the memory of my father

"Don't fear going slowly.
Fear only standing still."

—Ancient Chinese Proverb

Acknowledgments

There are many who had a role in helping me to realize this book: Christina Orth, for her friendship, support, and guidance; Maureen Orth, for her generosity regarding this project; K. C. Cole and Pat Murphy, two science writers, for their support and encouragement; Dr. Stephen A. Rothstein, for his help with research materials; Knox Burger, Kitty Sprague, and Katherine Preminger, for working to secure a publisher for my manuscript; Kathryn Court, my editor, and Caroline White, for helping me to turn that manuscript into a book; and the Exploratorium, for giving me the time to do so. I also thank the many women and men, too numerous to list here, who have taken the time to share their own personal stories with me.

Introduction

It was on Saint Valentine's Day, 1985, that I had my right breast removed. My mastectomy was absolute and my survival a relative certainty. I was single, aged thirty-four.

I realized that, as a single woman, I faced a greater emotional risk as I strived to reestablish my life after breast cancer. After all, the question "How do I make love with a man?" isn't clearly asked or answered in the medical literature. And I wanted to know how I would tell a total stranger, not my husband of twenty years, "Yes, I have had breast cancer and had my breast removed. And by the way, I think you are cute." I was thinking about the second date, not the second decade. But I knew there were women who were also perplexed and worried even though they had been married for many years.

I was in no way prepared for what had happened. There was

INTRODUCTION

no lump, no family history. Yet within two weeks of what I considered a routine visit for a breast exam, I had to give up my breast. And just as cancer destroyed my sense of invulnerability by threatening my life and survival, it also raised other questions about my future. I was young enough to still be grappling with the meaning of life. Now, suddenly, both its purpose and meaning seemed to hinge on my soon-to-be-severed breast.

I turned to books for information on treatment choices and the technical aspects of this disease. And I automatically looked to books for answers to my personal questions—the daunting issue of sex and my life as a single-breasted woman. I was shocked and unnerved to discover that I could not find a single book and not a single concrete and practical chapter within a book dealing with sexuality.

As is common after a mastectomy, I was visited by a Reach to Recovery volunteer. Reach to Recovery is a program in which survivors of breast cancer counsel, one on one, those newly faced with this disease. I requested a visit from a woman close to my own age.

My volunteer was a thirty-eight-year-old woman named Caroline. I questioned her about the saga of her own discovery, treatment, and recovery. We talked about reconstruction. Then I asked her how mastectomy affected her sex life. It was a rude shock to hear that her husband did nothing to her reconstructed breast. It angered me to think that a part of my body, even a missing or a reconstructed part, might be ignored. "I'll never put up with that," I said naively from my bed. And I wanted to know more. I wanted to know why her husband couldn't deal with it and why she let him ignore it. But Caroline was unprepared to answer my prying questions with anything

INTRODUCTION

more than vague and shy reassurances. I appreciated what she told me, but it just wasn't enough.

That conversation fanned my already burning desire to know more. I found an ongoing mastectomy support group, the only one available in San Francisco in 1985. It was made up of fifteen women who had undergone mastectomy and was led by a social worker. But the minute I walked in, my heart sank. I was the youngest woman there by far, and it seemed more of a tea party than a therapy session. I munched chocolate chip cookies for an hour, walked out, and never returned.

By now I was truly angry. I was angry with the popular literature on cancer. It was either technical or inspirational at a time when I was ready for something practical. I was angry with Reach to Recovery and the silence of the medical profession. I was angry with the networks of women working to support each other. I found them all strangely mute on the issues that were certainly as relevant to them as they were to me.

After all, the diagnosis and treatment of cancer are terrifying enough. But with no practical help available on the subject of sexuality, I felt completely abandoned. How could there be, in the mid-1980s, a total absence of information about cancer and sexuality in the channels most available to women after this crisis? Hadn't anybody else ever asked these questions? Weren't they implicit in every woman's deep-seated fear of breast cancer? Or was I crazy? I felt guilty about my seemingly solitary need to know. I couldn't have been more thankful to be alive. But I was also concerned about what being alive now meant. I could see the very same questions on the lips of my fellow patients, even in the eyes of my friends as they stared at me in my hospital bed. But nobody was talking.

It was only as recently as the 1970s that women like Shirley

INTRODUCTION

Temple Black, Betty Ford, and Happy Rockefeller felt free to speak openly about mastectomy for the first time. But what I discovered was that the moment had yet to arrive for women to also speak openly about mastectomy and sex. Even Betty Rollin in her excellent book *First, You Cry* merely alludes to it as she describes her post-mastectomy relationships. Not until the very last page does she muse aloud about what had become my exact dilemma—the prospect of making love with a new man. Clearly, I was of a new generation of women. I was young enough to recognize the taboo against discussing sex and mastectomy but also old enough to have the disease. I was of the generation that talked about sex. And I wanted and needed to know what others felt and did. I wanted step-by-step cinematic details.

It was certainly my great good fortune in bypassing chemotherapy and radiation that triggered the immediacy of my questions and, eventually, this book. I was angry at being thrown right back into life without a new set of rules by which to play the game. I had no choice but to go ahead with my life and get my own answers, unprepared. What follows is my personal experience, the ups and downs, the occasionally wrenching, sometimes funny, sometimes painful details of what I went through.

I wrote this book to provide the sort of information, guidance, and reassurance that I couldn't find about the quality of sexual life. Because I felt that what I really needed four years ago was the detailed experiences of other women, of those who had already experienced what I was about to face.

I have also written this book for me. Writing is one way of looking back in an effort to both chronicle and understand. This process has meant not just writing, but talking with other

INTRODUCTION

women about their experience as a way of comprehending and informing my own.

Among the women I spoke with, some were friends of friends, but most started out as strangers. Many I counseled when I became a Reach to Recovery volunteer in 1986. The women were married, single, and divorced, and of all ages and backgrounds. I sought women who were open, vocal, and willing to share intimate details with me as I tried to gain a sense of how others have coped with this disease. Some moved slowly and steadily toward their lives as single-breasted women. Others raced. And some have made no progress at all. So while this book recounts my own personal experience, it has clearly been sharpened and focused by these other conversations. The result is a book for and about all women faced with mastectomy, lumpectomy, radiation, and chemotherapy. It is about coming to terms with the psychosexual and, therefore, the emotional aftermath of this disease.

I found both writing this book and acting as a Reach to Recovery volunteer to be a moving experience. I worked with women as they waded through the most intense and devastating periods of their lives. At times, it forced me to relive my own diagnosis again and again—the shock, the confusion, and the fear that I was quite alone in my attempt to find answers.

Perhaps it was no accident, then, that in September 1987 I published an article in *Vogue* magazine called "Sex and the Single-Breasted Woman." It was a personal account and prompted quite a response at the time. Women called and wrote. Some called out of joy, because I gave expression to their feelings if not their actual experiences. My example motivated them, and even their husbands and boyfriends, to speak. Others called because, like me at the time of my di-

INTRODUCTION

agnosis, they had questions and fears and nowhere to turn. Many called because they were still lost or stuck, a long time after their first diagnosis and treatment. Each of these women seemed to welcome my example. They thanked me for offering concrete evidence of what some had struggled to learn and what others were aching to find out—that their emotional and physical life had not come to an end. Precisely because of these responses, this book has become a reality. They confirmed my belief that the time for a frank account of sexuality and breast cancer was overdue.

1

If I describe myself as streetwise it is because I grew up in the Bensonhurst section of Brooklyn, an area wedged between the Verrazano Bridge and Coney Island. It is only a few blocks southeast of Bay Ridge, the setting for John Travolta's movie *Saturday Night Fever*. Bensonhurst is a neighborhood of lower-middle-class Italians and Jews who live in row upon row of semi-detached brick two-family houses. The Italian-owned houses have red painted sidewalks, ornate ironwork on the screen doors, and statues of the Virgin Mary in the garden. But since we were Jewish, our house had only a tree out front. I lived with my mother, my father, my two sisters (Marcia, the eldest, nine years older than me, and Gale, who was seven years my senior), my maternal grandma Tillie, and the dog. My parents had been married only one year before Grandma

Tillie moved in, and this strong-willed and opinionated matriarch, to put it plainly, became a lifelong regent to my inexperienced mother's throne. The six of us—not counting Trooper—lived in six rooms.

By the time I was seven, my sister Marcia had already moved out of the house to attend Barnard College, all the way uptown, in Manhattan. Since Marcia attended a Seven Sisters college, she went down in family history as the brilliant daughter. Gale, being no fool, became the beautiful one. And she was. She had a string of boyfriends going back to sixth grade, when "Toodie," who was half her size, fell in love with her while harmonizing with the guys on the street corner. Later on, the greengrocer's son left watermelons tied in red ribbons on the front stoop as offerings of love. Next came stretch pants from a ski wear manufacturer's son, and eventually expensive jewelry from rich men abroad.

Meanwhile, I was developing my creative talents by playing with big white rolls of toilet paper instead of building blocks, and loving a bald and usually naked rubber doll passed down to me by my sisters. I often concocted mixtures of calamine lotion and other nefarious potions from the medicine chest by stirring them carefully in the bathroom sink, behind closed doors. Despite such private goings-on, the frontiers of my life were pretty much bounded by my mother, grandmother, and my sister Gale.

Shopping was my mother's passion. When I was eight, my mother went to work at a big department store on Forty-second Street in Manhattan. Every day, she'd emerge from the subway carrying a shopping bag full of marvelous bargains that were further reduced by her 20 percent employee discount. Usually, some of those goodies were for me. But if I was well dressed because my mother worked, I was also miffed. I had decided that I wasn't going to eat what my grandmother cooked for me in my mother's stead. I ate only pizza, ham sandwiches, and turkey TV dinners. But around five o'clock, I stood watch at the window waiting for my mother. "Hi, Mom. Did you bring me anything good?" I'd always ask.

My father worked six days a week, and by the time I reached third grade he was gone too. I don't mean that he left physically, but the limits and frustrations of his life weighed him down and he seemed to retreat into silence. I knew that my father was an intelligent and thoughtful man. I had heard stories from one of my uncles about how when Daddy was young, his teacher gave him money to enroll in college. But as the oldest of seven children, my father was able to attend college for only one year. He kept a ham radio and Morse coder in the basement, along with lots of electronic gadgets. It was obvious that he should have worked in science, computers or communications, but instead he sold TV sets. His main pleasure became the game of chess. I will always remember him hunched over his pieces, lost in thought, staring and silent.

Perhaps I grew up in the middle of his mid-life crisis. Because suddenly, at the onset of my adolescence, when my father turned fifty, he seemed to come out of it and come back to me after all those years. He had gotten a new job, working as a chemist. But a few months later, on his way to work, my father died on the street from a heart attack. I was fourteen. I knew that things had seriously changed. In one fell swoop my father was dead, my grandmother seemed old enough to be an infant herself, my mother was on her own for the first time, and I had to grow up. After half a year my mother began dating, and within another six months she married a man I automatically despised.

When you grow up in New York City, you grow up on the

streets. I hung out with a crowd of girls and boys. The girls were college bound. The guys, on the other hand, were lucky if they graduated from high school. They were mostly tough and worldly wise, sitting around planning car battery thefts and other petty crime. I liked their crude knowledge of life, their smarts, their rough charm, the fact that they owned cars and knew how to fix them and that they were oddly protective and considerate. I didn't quite know what they liked about me, but I think my large breasts had something to do with it. Because at age fourteen, I was very amply endowed. They called me "Buns" or "Bunnie" and I know it wasn't my behind they were talking about. In those days, my breasts seemed quite large and were a source of burdensome attention. I both despised the spotlight—feeling singled out and angry to the point of tears—and came to expect it.

My high school graduation present from my sister Gale was an airplane ticket around the world. Gale was twenty-four, I was seventeen. We went to Europe first, then the Middle East and on to Africa. In each place, I was overwhelmed by the attentions of foreign men. They promised to teach me things in England, to clear up my skin (if only I would make love) in France, and in one very frightening instance in Turkey, actually threatened to rape me. In Africa, they offered to take me on long rides down dark deserted beaches. I passed for twenty-four in the company of my sister, but my eyes betrayed me. I seemed brash and confident, but I was terrified when it came to men.

On the day that I returned to Bensonhurst from abroad, my mother's new husband died. His children did not attend the funeral and neither did I. I hated the man. But I cried over the fact that their father had died, because I was still looking for one to love.

UP FRONT

I lived at home with my mother and started school just a bus ride away at Brooklyn College. I discovered art history and embraced literature. I spoke French, worked hard, and spent long hours reading nineteenth-century novels on the rust-colored club chair in the front room. I was conscious but afraid of my burgeoning sexuality. It had little outlet except for slightly suggestive stories written under the watchful eye of a handsome young writing professor. And his watchful eye made me uncomfortable too. To put it simply, I did not pass into womanhood gracefully. I fought and I struggled against it until I found Ari at age nineteen.

We met in Miami. I was one of the many college students there for spring vacation. Ari was twenty, but had quit school. When he smiled at me, I stopped dead in my tracks. Ari wasn't just handsome, he was beautiful. He was a smiling Mediterranean god with a perfect face encased in wild curls.

Beneath Ari's sensual good looks was a sweet and simple personality. I liked his common sense. I was drawn to him as I had been attracted to the boys on the street corner in Brooklyn. He was so different from me. I was self-protective and bookish. He wasn't afraid of feeling or risk. So when I was nineteen, after I had skirted the issue for years, Ari became my first lover, and he remained my boyfriend for the next four years.

I graduated from college and from Ari at the same time. I was offered a fellowship to study literature at Washington University in Saint Louis. I had decided to get a Ph.D., just like my oldest sister, only Marcia was now a clinical psychologist, living in England with her husband and two kids. But like her, I took my first step by leaving Brooklyn for an academic career.

The university offered to pay me full tuition plus money to live on, and I didn't ask any questions. But I quickly discovered that I couldn't adjust to Saint Louis. From my intensely urban point of view, it was a small town. In fact, it was suburban. And as a non-driving New Yorker I felt utterly stranded. So I studied, I taught, and I banged my head against the wall when I thought the airport was snowed in at Christmas. After two years and a master's degree, I had had enough of life in the Midwest. So at the age of twenty-four I moved to San Francisco, where my sister Gale lived. I had heard it had a real downtown and public transportation—all the things I needed without having to return to New York.

I had left behind the comfortable structure of school and home, though I softened the blow by moving to the same city as Gale. In fact, I slept on her living-room floor for three months until I found a job. But the minute I found work, I got my own apartment, near Chinatown, on the other side of town. Despite Gale's generosity, I was already feeling under her thumb. We hadn't lived together for years, but in the first month an old pattern that had been playing itself out since childhood reemerged. On the one hand, she offered me whatever I needed. But without warning, she withdrew her support. I was no longer a child, and it was time for me to assert my independence from my middle sister. A year later, Gale moved to southern California.

I spent my time in San Francisco building strong friendships with women but slipped in and out of uncertain romantic relationships. Often alone, I hung out in my dining room night after winter night, close to the heater, listening to the Chinese motorcycle gang practice karate in platform shoes upstairs.

In those moments, I found the beauty of San Francisco painful. I moved even deeper into Chinatown, since the crowded streets, the smell, the noise reminded me of home. And I kept myself busy by learning photography, writing what

UP FRONT

I considered inspired art criticism for a local publication called *Artweek* at five dollars a crack, and becoming another of those attractive young women whom I ran into at the bargain matinees on Saturday afternoons. I went to the movies to escape the California sunshine, I think.

Given all those Saturdays, it doesn't surprise me that I eventually fell for a movie star type, a man who was as handsome and sophisticated as Cary Grant. In fact, Brian was a bluish-blood businessman. Once every few weeks, dressed in a cashmere suit and Gucci loafers, he would drop in at the Art Institute, where I worked, and stare at me along with the art.

He was seventeen years my senior and divorced, and he talked to me about things like responsibility and planning. I didn't understand half of what he said, but gradually I came to invest in the stock market, drive his boat, and learn how to ski. He introduced me to California. I started to hike, noticed the changes in the tides, and learned to recognize the flowers, the birds, and the fish. I even began to use the car I had bought. I considered getting an MBA. Sometimes on weekends, I shared him with his youngest daughter. I was fascinated to observe the two of them together, for I had never really seen a father and daughter together before. And although Michelle was eight and I was in my late twenties, Brian plied us both with fatherly advice.

After three years, I had gained self-confidence, thanks to Brian's testimonies to my beauty and the emotional security he afforded me. But we were at different points in our lives. From the perspective of an unsettled thirty-year-old, Brian seemed increasingly predictable and conservative. It was the little things that got me, such as repeating the same jokes or referring to certain films as "women's movies."

Brian had predicted that when I turned thirty I would want a change—commitment and babies. But in the end, it wasn't commitment I wanted. I crudely said that I didn't want to stick around until I had to push him around in a wheelchair. I broke up with Brian, found a new job, and felt my life open up.

I had never seen anything like the Exploratorium. When I first entered its dark and cavernous space, lights and sounds flashed and flickered. Even the lights from the offices were like spaceship windows, floating as they did in the otherwise dark and chaotic museum. The exhibits were improvised experiments constructed to reveal natural phenomena in the everyday world, and the whole place was infused with a spirit of creativity that captured the best of both science and art. I had come to see Frank Oppenheimer, the famous and eccentric physicist who founded the place. Frank was the brother of J. Robert Oppenheimer, the "father" of the atom bomb. Frank sometimes referred to himself as its "uncle," since he too worked on that world-altering project.

Frank's big black dog was sleeping in the office when I walked in. Then Frank walked in, and I noticed his dazzling blue eyes and energetic yet frail body. He carried a cane, which he beat on the ground and twirled in the air like a drum majorette. As he talked to me, he spun around the office, walked out, and then back in again, making it impossible for me to hear what he said. Half the time he talked to the wall and rubbed his head, massaging his thoughts. "We need an annual report," I heard him say. "I don't write annual reports," I countered. But for some reason he hired me. My job was to write about the museum in a variety of ways, but I spent much of my time responding to requests from the press, since the international media had discovered the wonders of the Exploratorium.

To work at the Exploratorium was to work rough-and-ready, low tech, and on the cheap. Two or three of us shared each small office. But there was always time to get excited by some idea or some new gizmo and to gather round it and figure out how it worked. In this way, we managed to teach and to learn from each other.

Because Frank had started the museum with his family, it was run like a mom-and-pop grocery store, even though the family now exceeded one hundred employees in their twenties and thirties. Frank was certainly still in charge. He encouraged us to scream at each other if we were angry, but also to be friends and to get to know the intimate details of each other's lives. So business meetings were often the equivalent of sitting around the dinner table and arguing over who was going to get the biggest allowance. Although our work areas had no natural daylight, no fresh air, and no privacy, there was a mystique and commitment that made our work as important as the other parts of our lives. And in such an environment many close relationships were formed, even deep friendships and love affairs. Several couples met and married and began raising babies at the Exploratorium; over the years various combinations of friends and lovers moved together and apart, although rarely away.

Such was the case for Uwe and me. Uwe is German, a physicist and a science exhibit designer, one of a continual flow of professionals that come to the Exploratorium from all around the world. Uwe is six-foot-nine, with long blond hair and piercing blue eyes. He appeared one day and began bounding past my door on his way to the coffee machine. A week or two later, when I came back from lunch, I found him sitting at my desk using my telephone, bellowing into the receiver in Hebrew. A German speaking Hebrew? I was immediately intrigued, and more importantly, I was wondering who had paid for the call. I scowled at him.

But Uwe was delighted. At long last, after weeks and weeks in have-a-nice-day-California, he was confronted with the slightly abrasive charm that had inspired him to move from Germany to Israel. Uwe took to drinking excessive amounts of coffee just so he could walk by my office and chat. Frank came by too, spinning in circles on his cane. He was watching our burgeoning friendship, a rather obvious new development in international museum relations.

Uwe spoke four languages, and even in English his sharp mind was quite evident. Out of nowhere, he said one day that he hadn't fallen in love yet. "That is everything," he told me in his direct way. His unexpected comment seemed as much an invitation as a simple declaration and it played over and over in my head.

We spent two months together in San Francisco. Then we carried on a five-month monogamous long-distance affair by mail and telephone until we finally met in person once again—this time in the Middle East. When I arrived, Uwe seemed happy to see me. But his unrestrained pleasure lasted for only one day. The fact was that despite all his long-distance hopefulness, I had gotten too close to suit him. In all my other relationships I had been the one to back away. But gradually I had to admit that Uwe was the one saying no to me in a thousand different ways. Despite the sultry Middle Eastern air with its smell of grapefruit and orange blossoms everywhere, I saw that Uwe was afraid and that there would be no real love between us. Things had not worked out, he told me at the end of my two months' stay, but we could still be friends. I hardly agreed. Yet there was a painful complication: Uwe had accepted a permanent job at the Exploratorium and was going to relocate to San Francisco.

I cried all the way to London. I stopped there to visit my sister Marcia on my way home. When I stepped off the plane, she greeted me, "You look so healthy and tanned!" But I felt as wrung out and gray as the English weather. We had only a few days together. When the time came for Marcia to return home to Warwickshire, I started to cry uncontrollably. I had borne the separation from Uwe, but it was too much to give up my sister so soon as well. "I want to go home with you," I sobbed. So Marcia packed me into her car along with the suitcases. For two days I sat by the fireplace in her big house. I had planned to spend my time soaking up the English culture, but I soaked up the comfort of my English family instead.

I knew I was going to need even more in the way of emotional reinforcement when I got back to San Francisco. And not unlike my mother when she met her new husband, I seized my first opportunity. A friend of a friend, a man named Bill, phoned me one day out of the blue. "I've been told that I have to meet you," he said. And I carelessly and selfishly wrapped myself in Bill's attention as if it were a suit of mail. He was my protection. Because a few months after my return home, Uwe was back. I saw him at work every day. In the many months that followed, I often railed against his torturous presence. Why did he have to come back to San Francisco? I asked. The answer was all too soon in coming. I would need Uwe's strength as one of my main supports in facing the terrifying specter of cancer.

2

"Dr. Elliot called. Call back in 15 minutes" read the pink message slip on my desk. And from that very first moment I began to tremble. The doctor had told me just two days earlier that he would call only if there was a problem. "Probably nothing to worry about," he had said.

Nothing to worry about. No family history. No prior illnesses, no hospitalizations. Strong and sturdy. Only 18 percent body fat. I was a cliché of contemporary fitness despite my intellectual pretensions and a heavy dose of natural cynicism.

It was my new friend Bill who told me to get my breasts checked. "You've been complaining for a month," he said. "If you'll get your breasts checked, I'll have the warts on my penis removed." How could I argue with that?

But what Bill said startled me, because he was right. I did

complain a lot after we worked out together at the athletic club. Sometimes I would actually hold on to my breasts to relieve the aching.

I made an appointment at a breast-screening clinic. It turned out the soreness was directly related to my workouts. Yet the nurse found a slight thickening at about twelve o'clock, above the nipple on the right-hand side. I found out later that what you feel on one side and fail to feel on the other is by definition suspicious. "It's probably nothing," the nurse said. "But a surgeon will want to do a fine needle aspiration just to be sure." I thought she was going to send me home, but instead she was making arrangements for an immediate evaluation. Oh, I knew I was okay. But as I waited for the procedure to begin, I was starting to feel scared.

The surgeon slipped a fine needle into my breast and removed some fluid. "Probably nothing to worry about," he said. I walked out of his office and saw a woman I knew slightly. She too seemed to be clutching her breast.

"My mother died of breast cancer and I'm terrified," Ann told me. "I had a biopsy and it's okay, but I came here for a second opinion to be sure. Your doctor is very good."

I was glad to hear it. But secretly I was shocked that she was so concerned about this disease. For the first time, I really understood what I had only read about. Breast cancer is a concern for millions of women. I held on to my good health tenaciously, but there was already a perceptible weakness in my grip. With one visit to the doctor, my immunity to the ravages of disease had weakened. I know because driving home, up and down the San Francisco hills, I started to cry.

And I was already angry. How dare cancer even falsely implicate me? There were sick people to be cared for. I was okay and I resented this case of temporary mistaken identity.

"And yet," I consoled myself, "I've learned how *other* women must worry and suffer."

Then, a few days later, I saw the phone message from Dr. Elliot and I knew.

Ginny was the first person I saw. She had her coat on and was on her way past my office door and out of the museum, home to her husband and kids. I yelled, "I think I have cancer." Ginny looked stunned. She came into my office, took off her coat, and sat down. "Sometimes they call back to tell you good news," she said. But Ginny was wrong.

"I'm as surprised as you to have to tell you this," the doctor said. "I'm sorry to have to say that the test showed malignancy."

All I remember is the word *malignancy*. I wondered what it would be like to hear that news, and now it was happening. I just gasped and covered my mouth with my hand.

"Come in tomorrow and we will discuss your options. And bring someone along who can help you decide. You will have a lot of questions. Get a pencil and paper and start writing them down. See my secretary at nine A.M. and have her arrange for a chest X ray, a blood test, and a mammogram," he said.

That was it. The test showed malignancy. With those words, I was left to struggle with the news of cancer in that funny time between the end of work and evening.

Ginny told me she'd accompany me to the doctor if I needed her. But Ginny wasn't the person I was looking for. I got up and started roaming from office to office. I saw my friend Wendy.

"Wendy, it's malignant," I said.

"What is?" she asked. "You mean Frank?" Because at seventy-two, Frank Oppenheimer had himself developed cancer.

"Me," I said and kept walking.

I was searching the museum for Uwe. He was the only person big enough to protect me from the news. But he had already gone home. I went back to my office and called him.

"Hallo," Uwe said into the telephone. His voice booms over a telephone the way his body fills a doorway.

"I've had some bad news," I said.

"What bad news?"

"I found out I have breast cancer." I was like a ten-year-old awkwardly rehearsing that line for the school play.

"I come over right away," he said. When I hung up I saw a note from Wendy under the door. "Call me if you want company," it said in her skinny little scrawl.

I walked out of my office again, and was drawn into a cozy room, full of low lights and an odd assortment of mirrors, patterns, colors, and other tools for teaching kids. I saw Lynn packing up.

"Lynn, I just had some bad news," I said.

"What?" she asked.

"Breast cancer." I was trying to get used to the line.

"You can't drive home," she said, shocked.

Her reaction seemed odd. "Why, because I have breast cancer?" I asked. It seemed plausible.

So in the end we compromised and Lynn sat in her car while I drove, passing hundreds of cars with hundreds of people going out to have a good time. It seemed implausible that life could still be so frivolous for everyone else. But I only had to look down at my turquoise shoes to prove that I had been equally frivolous only an hour before.

Uwe was there, waiting outside my house when Lynn dropped me off. There was something new in all this, something awful and terrible, but also pleasant. I was suddenly not alone.

Uwe and I hadn't spoken in weeks and now I was too much

in shock to have anything to say. So we dealt with the news of my cancer by going to a restaurant. I seemed to float above it all—his company, hunger, waiting for a table, and cancer. I floated above the restaurant's red leather booths full of animated people talking about career moves and real estate deals and what seemed like all the odd preoccupations of the well and the living.

I felt distant from my surroundings, but I needed physical closeness. When I was seated across the table from Uwe, I immediately thought that he was too far away. So I silently crossed over to his side of the table and leaned on him, a man whom I wanted dearly to love. I had dragged my feelings for him across two continents not long before. But if I harbored any more of those fantasies, they shattered at about the same instant that I read that pink message slip. Cancer is demanding. It requires honesty. Uwe was not my husband or even my boyfriend or whatever was required at times like this. But I felt I needed him more than anyone else I knew, and I said something about it to him.

"I am here and will continue to be here as a pure gesture," Uwe told me. I thanked him. I needed him to help me face the cancer.

The next day I was assaulted by blood tests and X rays before I ever saw the doctor. A clerk took my forms and asked, "Are you pre-op?"

What could she mean? I had come to talk about options with the doctor. Wouldn't something clean and neat, like radiation, work? I had already decided surgery was out of the question.

"Are you pre-op?" another clerk asked me when I showed up for X rays. I felt like an immigrant at Ellis Island. I was about to be deported but I couldn't speak the language in order to protest.

"I jogged four miles yesterday!" I wanted to shout.

"Are you pre-op?" they kept asking. It was their code for cancer. It was their code for not-a-visitor, not-a-friend-who-did-the-driving, but the one with the disease who *would* be pre-op, just you wait and see.

I wished Uwe was there with me, but I had been afraid of involving him too much. He had so many strong opinions, he might have made my decision for me. Instead I had asked my sister Gale to accompany me. She had just finished law school and was back in the San Francisco area. But Gale was under tremendous pressure of her own. She was studying for the bar exam, an experience that my sudden crisis rendered one of the worst of her life. I asked Gale along because she was family. Family had rights to decisions about my body somehow. And since Gale was training to become a lawyer, I expected her mind to be sharp.

Dr. Elliot wrote notes for us as he talked. He provided a mini-course in breast cancer—its implications and its treatment. Breast cancer the local illness, and breast cancer the systemic illness. Percentages-of-survival rates at five and ten years for courses of treatment one, two, and three—namely, mastectomy, lumpectomy with radiation, and a wide excision without radiation. Chemotherapy might be required later. I was stunned.

Mastectomy? Survival rates at five and ten years? Was he talking to me?

"Ten years seems like next week," I said. "In ten years I'll only be forty-four. A baby." You don't talk to people about living five or ten more years. We just live until we're old.

Linda Dackman

So now, even the doctor, with his wing-tipped shoes, blue eyes, and engaging overbite smile, was telling me the same thing as the clerks. I was pre-op. Impossible. I rejected the notion of a systemic illness and a shortened life. There was only so much that I could absorb at one time.

I was already drowning in the flood of percentages. How many survive for how long with this size lesion? How many show positive lymph nodes and evidence of "spread"? The numbers washed over me and I began sinking in the inevitability of the odds. It all seemed as well organized, efficient, and terrifying as a fast-food franchise.

Dr. Elliot told me I had an 80 percent chance of survival over the next ten years, and I knew he thought he was giving me good news. Eighty percent? It was shattering. I wasn't going to live forever?

My mortality was impossible. And being 20 percent short of all my friends was enraging. How dare he speak to me of intervals as short as ten years? After all, I was a slow starter in life, barely out of the gate when I was thirty. How dare he change the rules midway into my turtle race?

To fend off the effect of his words, I asked millions of questions. Some of my questions were obvious and natural. But most of them were academic and overly objective. I was protecting myself with my fascination for the medical process. I was pretending it was not my illness. Suddenly, I was a journalist, but I was covering my own demise.

I became bright and charming and curious and delightful and, most of all, detached. My sister Gale, on the other hand, said almost nothing. I could see she felt the impact of the doctor's words much more than I did. She realized that he was talking about the survival chances of her baby sister. But I felt she didn't understand what the doctor was saying. She wasn't asking the right questions. I was the only one listening, trying to decide. But if I responded like an "A" student to the facts of my disease, it was only because, while I understood everything the doctor said, I hadn't felt a thing.

Just two hours later, my protective wall began to crumble. I sent Gale home and I went through the hospital mill of more waiting rooms and further tests alone. I was cold and angry, sitting in a shroud of a hospital gown answering the same questions over and over. At one point a woman doctor, a radiologist, entered the room. She was the first woman doctor I had seen all day, and I jumped on her, appealing to her woman to woman. "What would you do in my case?"

She hesitated. "Dr. Elliot is an excellent doctor. I would go to him if I had breast cancer. Your area looks manageable to me—a partial should be enough without radiation."

"But Dr. Elliot seems to be pushing for mastectomy," I said.

Despite the discrepancy, for a moment this woman doctor made me feel brighter. She seemed to think I could preserve my breast and also avoid minor doses of the A-bomb. For at least the second time that day, I thought I had made a decision. But the facts and my decisions kept changing.

They told me to call at 4:15 to discuss the mammograms, but I planted myself outside Dr. Elliot's office to discuss them in person. I didn't want to leave. This place was the wellspring of information.

I must have had the look of the newly indicted on my face—pallid horror, a certain vacancy. The woman beside me spoke. She was in her mid-thirties, overweight, and excitable. "Why are you here?" she asked. I told her.

"I've already had my mastectomy," she said.

I looked. I couldn't tell. "How did you decide what to do?" I asked.

"I was just petrified," she said. "There was no other choice for me. I just wanted it out, off, the safest thing as fast as possible."

She ranted, gestured. She told me how she liked to drink beer with her friends, so she was overweight and that was bad for cancer. How lucky she is to be so uninhibited, I thought. No apparent anguish or angst about the treatment on top of the disease. But of course, she was terrified. She was trying to convince herself and me that her breast was really off and that she had done the right thing. She had made her choice. Now she was trying to live with it.

A tall, attractive blond woman sitting across the room put down her magazine. "I'm having reconstruction," she said.

"You are?" I marveled. She looked so fashionable and attractive I couldn't believe she had anything unusual going on under her clothes.

"I've had both my breasts reconstructed," she told me. She was reassuringly blithe about the whole thing, as if the operation and the visits and the cancer were unfortunate annoyances. I wanted to know why she felt so undaunted.

"Can I ask you a favor? Will you let me see your breasts?" I asked.

"Sure," she said.

We went into an examination room. I passed Dr. Elliot as I followed her down the hall. I waved and said, "She's showing me her breasts," as if I was on my way to buy my first vanilla ice-cream cone.

When Rory undressed, I felt a rush of pleasure. She looked fantastic in her silk-and-lace slip. All I could see was the upper skin of round, firm breasts—no evidence of reconstruction on either side. "You see," she said, "you can even wear a bikini." Her breasts looked better than mine through her braless slip. They didn't need any support.

But when she slipped the garment off her shoulders, I was taken aback. Her right breast, reconstructed ten years before, was not beautiful. It had several scars and changes in coloration due to skin grafting. But the breast itself, as a form, seemed marvelous from an engineering point of view. It was dome-shaped and firm—something like an upside-down soup bowl with a nipple sitting in the center. "May I touch it?" I asked. It felt soft but strong, not terribly alien—not like concrete, wood, or even beanbaggy.

With nothing much to compare it to, that reconstructed breast looked pretty good. Rory's left side was still in the earliest phase of inflation, part of a new, more immediate reconstruction process. A long diagonal scar ran from the center of her rib cage up toward her armpit and right through the center of her still-unformed left breast. Rory called it her "grapefruit corsage"—a kind of water-bed mound in the chest. These were the odd tribal markings of mastectomy.

Rory was a young grandmother in her fifties, but she seemed younger to me, laughingly extolling the benefits of reconstructed breasts, because they don't bounce in aerobics class. Then she told me that her kids said, "Hey, Mom, you look like a boy," when they saw her after her first mastectomy. "My husband told me he didn't marry me for my breasts. Really, it's not that bad. You know, I bought a business on the day that I went into the hospital," she said. "Just don't let it stop you" were her parting words.

When all the other patients had gone, I sat down with Dr. Elliot again. He placed my mammograms on a viewing screen. "Bad news," he said. "The mammogram shows something bigger than what we felt." He pulled out a little plastic ruler. "Five and a half centimeters of calcification. That's fairly large. It practically disqualifies you from any options besides a mastectomy. Five and a half centimeters is pushing it. I would recommend mastectomy."

The facts—and the solutions—kept changing.

But now I had seen a reconstructed breast, or, more accurately, an undaunted reconstructed person. I was inspired by her example and I decided that if I had to have it done, then I too could live with it. I imagined that I would be temporarily inconvenienced by the operation and I would end up with a not-my-own but nevertheless perfectly matched breast.

I had no real understanding of the doctor's information, either regarding mastectomy or my prognosis. Nor did I understand the limits of reconstruction. All I focused on was my momentary consolation—that I might end up with *Gidget Goes Hawaiian* breasts. I had no conception of what it would take to get there. It wasn't so much that my information or understanding was shallow. It just hadn't sunk in.

Uwe was draped across his motorcycle in front of my house when I got home, holding a parking space for me. I was thrilled to see him. It was the first time in years that I parked my car without circling Nob Hill for twenty minutes. But it was much more than that. I was elated by my encounter with Rory, feeling as if even mastectomy was not the end of my world. And here was Uwe, waiting for me.

"I went to find you in the hospital, but I couldn't remember your doctor's name."

"Oh," I said, "Dr. Elliot. But how come you're not working?"

"I couldn't work. I'm too worried. I've been sitting here for three hours."

"It's going to be okay. I can live with a mastectomy if I have to," I said.

My spirits were very good and Uwe didn't upset me with questions about the details. Instead, we drove over to Wendy's for dinner. I sat and read my health insurance policy, while Uwe and Wendy leafed through a book I bought at the medical center on women's options in the treatment of breast cancer.

It didn't start to gel in my own mind until the next day. I called Ruth, the breast-screening nurse who first discovered my lump. Suddenly, I had questions. "I will try to answer you honestly," she told me.

"Do the five and a half centimeters on the mammogram increase my likelihood of lymph node involvement?"

"You are making all the right connections. From a statistical point of view, yes. But not everyone conforms to what the statistics indicate."

Her confirmation shook me. I didn't even hear the rest. I had already sunk under the wave of new realization and fear. I began to tremble. But before I could dial again, the phone rang. And it kept ringing all day. I talked myself into a state of temporary comfort.

In the evening, I stretched out on the brown velvet couch in my living room with the glow from the brass pole lamp warming me. Diligently, I opened the book that Wendy and Uwe had been looking at the day before. It was time to read about treatment options and the course of the disease. I expected to read through it progressively, like a novel, taking in every last word. Only I lost patience with the book immediately. I didn't need to read the chapters on detection; I already knew I had cancer. My question was "What does having it mean?" So I checked the index. I found a table. There it was, succinctly stated. Five and a half centimeters. Stage III: 45 percent survival rate at ten years and probable lymph node involvement. I quickly determined that my odds had slipped 35 percent in the few hours between my first and second meetings with Dr. Elliot. I closed the book but I couldn't stop the whole new wave of realization and fear that followed. As I sat there, my resolve and strength seemed to evaporate. I had learned more than enough.

I began pacing the room. I was trembling. I decided to call my sister Marcia. It was exactly as it had been twenty years earlier. Then, at age fourteen, I called Marcia all by myself to tell her that our father had suddenly died of a heart attack. Then as now, it was a horrible thrill and also a relief to share the bad news.

Then Bill called, and a few others. It was close to midnight and I still needed someone. I wanted my friends around, but particularly Wendy and Uwe, the two people I knew who were strong and independent models for me. I called Uwe. He wasn't home. Why wasn't he home? Why wasn't he standing by for me? I left a message on his answering machine. I called Wendy. She was out. Yet I asked none of those questions about Wendy. I had to remind myself that they were both just friends.

I finally reached Wendy. All I had to do was say her name. The panic was clearly in my voice. "Do you want me to come over?" she asked and then, without pausing, said, "I'll be right there."

Once I put down the telephone I began to wail. I cried in loud, deep sobs that racked my whole body, muttering, "Why, why?" and "Oh, God." I had never cried like that before in my life—those wails—so total and so deep that the cries themselves were frightening. I knew that I might be, could be, dying. I had cancer.

Wendy arrived at one in the morning in her purple sweatshirt and leopard long underwear. Wendy is small and delicate, artistic and gentle. She looked funny in my kitchen alongside the giant, blond, and always talkative Uwe. He had showed up—staunch and persuasive—as soon as he got my message.

I wanted them both there because I felt as exposed as an infant. Together Uwe and Wendy seemed to fulfill my totally naked desire for love, nurturance, and security.

At Uwe's suggestion, the three of us began to look through my book describing the facts and the treatment of cancer, sometimes reading it out loud. We had long discussions about the statistics in the book, and Uwe kept telling me that whatever the numbers said, no matter how bad it seemed, I must make it my business to just be among those who survive. "You are only one and you have to be the one that makes it," he said. I wasn't sure whether I could will such a thing, whether I had as much will as Uwe seemed to possess.

He and I became like two lawyers arguing the case for my survival. It was an odd avenue toward emotional well-being, this rather rational and intellectual refutation of the significance and validity of numbers. But it seemed to work. The sharpness of Uwe's mind and the sheer force of his lungs wore down my fear of the possible spread of the disease. He harped on the theme of positive outlook, insisting I decide to "lick it" the way that I knew he would fight with every inch of his being. Wendy didn't say much. She listened with me to Uwe and then got up and started to bake bran muffins in the middle of the night.

The next day, the clarity of my resolve dimmed. There was a constant swing in my emotions; conversation and companionship were necessary to steady me. I was like a prizefighter in training, needing a coach to direct, motivate, talk to, and support me. Uwe became my coach and he held me at those times when the trembling was uncontrollable. And when I called my mother.

"Hi, how are you?" she asked.

"I guess I'm not that well, Mom."

"What do you mean, not well? What's the matter?"

"I found out that I have breast cancer."

That line still sounded so unnatural. I was telling my mother that her baby—her youngest daughter—had breast cancer. I knew that the whole family still held out faint hopes that I might find some guy that I could stand and who could stand me. They held out hopes of my producing the odd cousin for my sister Marcia's two sons. But not a new boyfriend, not even a date, not a new job, not a raise nor a successful investment nor world news was I calling about. Instead I was announcing a chronic disease of unknown dimensions.

"What are you telling me?" my mother cried. Instantly, I felt my mother's fear and insecurity, shock and self-doubt. I needed my mother. But I saw that what I needed was hard for her. Then she told me she would fly out.

"We'll come out" is what she said.

My mother had married again, and, this time at least, I liked her husband. But when I heard her turn to him and say, "You'll go?" I broke in immediately.

"Mom, listen Mom, I want you to come alone," I said through the weeping on both sides. I wanted my mother to come care for me during my recuperation, but I wanted only her—there was no question about that. The feeling was dark and deep; I still seethed over her marrying a strange man nearly twenty years before, so soon after my father's death. It had seemed to deny her love and support at a time when I needed it most. And now I saw it happening again. I saw her fear of coping alone rise up. It threatened to keep her from me when, on a most primitive level, I again wanted her all to myself. But now I was old enough to demand and get what I needed. In fact, cancer made it imperative for me.

I wanted to say, "Mom, I have cancer, come help me," and fall into her arms, but first I had to argue.

"Why can't Sol come along? He'll be a help," she said. She had to have someone else to rely on. But I had to say no. I had to say no several times until my mother could understand what I needed.

The next day, I called my mother for a calmer discussion of the facts and of what should take place. She seemed more in control, and was trying to be clear and direct as she spoke to me. She had talked to both my sisters, and that seemed to make a difference in her understanding of what her role should be. I told her to come after the surgery. I wanted her with me when there was something for her to do.

"And you don't think Sol should come?" she added, right near the end of our conversation.

"Mom!" I snapped.

"Okay, okay."

Gale, on the other hand, always seemed to know what I wanted and often went out of her way to give it to me. But this time, Gale was torn between the bar exam and the demands of family loyalty. And it was obvious that I was resentful no matter which way she turned. Because I had learned that, for all her generosity, Gale usually exacted a steep price. She alternated between control and cherishing, depending on her many needs and whims. And nothing had changed much. I couldn't help loving her, but if I got too close, I felt a self-preserving instinct to keep my distance.

Marcia said she would fly in from England if I wanted her to. I appreciated her offer, but I held it in reserve. For the moment, that seemed too much to ask.

Without acknowledging it, I had decided to cope without the direct emotional support of my family. After all, I had been on my own for thirteen years. I had developed a mechanism, as many who live thousands of miles from home do, of creating a family of friends. In the end, that family was what I most fully relied on.

On the last weekend before the surgery, Uwe and I drove to the Marin headlands, just over the Golden Gate Bridge. We walked down to a deserted beach. I watched the waves come in and break, turning over and over with a rhythm and power that was both reassuring and crushing. Their constant motion didn't stop or change in deference to me. My only consolation was their beauty, watching them until the incoming tide almost totally swallowed my narrow stretch of sand.

On the day I was due at the hospital, I scheduled an appointment with my therapist, Sam. I wanted to talk to him before facing the loss of my breast.

Sam asked me if I was angry.

"Yes," I said.

"If you're angry, why don't you scream?" he asked.

But I sat there silent, except for my rapidly beating heart and my fast breathing. Sam told me to pay attention to the effect my silence had on my body, and I noticed that it had quieted itself. "First the meager physical signs of anger disappear," he pointed out, "then so do the feelings."

That frightened me. I thought about all the other episodes of anger I had swallowed, probably in just that way. Had I internalized it? Was that the cause of my breast cancer? So I screamed loudly, I thought. Sam said the screams were shallow, empty. I repeated them over and over again until a scream flowed out of me with the force of a fireplace bellows being emptied of air. "Get out! Get out!" I screamed and cried at the cancer. I was screaming because my life depended on it.

I entered the hospital holding on to Uwe with one hand and holding a tiny charm, a carved wooden bird for good luck, in the other. I was frightened of the unknown procedures to take place the next morning, but I was curious about everything else. I felt as if I had won a terrible contest and now I was on a bizarre vacation. There was much to be distracted by, the push-button bed with the back and knee adjustments, the workings of the nurses stations, the relationship between doctors and nurses, the rounds of the medical students and interns and the questions that they all asked. I kept Uwe beside me as I took it all in. At first I refused to put on the hospital gown. After all, I was not really a patient.

Many friends came that night. One came bearing a basket of fresh oranges. Bill sent a dozen roses from Chicago, where he had been called away on business. Gale was there. Brian walked in looking handsome but tense. The oldest of all my friends, he looked the most worried. His face seemed to say that it wasn't so clear anymore who would be pushing whom around in a wheelchair. Everyone looked strangely drawn and concerned except Wendy. She arrived with a large glass vase and an exotic collection of one-of-a-kind flowers: orchids, anthurium, waxy Hawaiian and African blooms. She took a razor blade out of her purse and silently trimmed the stem bottoms and spent half an hour arranging the flowers until she got it right. One flower in particular smelled like paradise. It was the smell of peace and heaven. I planned to sleep with it under my nose. And so people kept coming and going until I was able to pretend that I was a harried executive, torn between my appointments and the telephone.

At long last an intern could wait no longer to examine me. He sent my friends into the hallway. After the examination I put on my ballet slippers, slipping them over turquoise anklet socks with black, yellow, and pink stripes. My socks were all that I had left of my street clothes. I walked out to the hallway holding my short hospital gown closed in the back.

"I'm done," I called out, a little like Alice afraid to venture back through the looking glass.

Uwe looked down at me from his great height. "You look beautiful," he said. "You look like a child."

I was. I was vulnerable, tiny, and fragile after only ten minutes in a hospital gown.

The phone stopped ringing when the switchboard closed, and by the time the lights had dimmed, only Uwe, Wendy, and I were left in the room. They sat on my bed and we talked until midnight. We tried to keep our voices low, but Uwe didn't really know how to whisper. He kept me afloat on the flood of his words. He talked away my fears like a salesman. "Yes, there is something. Yes, it will come off. But what it means to your life is up to you, is up to your attitude. If it were me, there would be no question. I would just survive.

"Life itself," he told me, "it's so wonderful. You have many friends. You are not alone. Forget about the numbers. The numbers mean nothing. You have only to worry about you. You just have to stay where you are, which is right here on earth."

In her own way, Wendy simply promised that she would make me more bran muffins.

I did not take the sleeping pill the nurse left. I settled myself in a straight line on the bed, flat on my back—practicing to be a patient anesthetized on a table. I examined the curves of my body, trying to assure myself that I was psychologically prepared for what would come next. I was saying good-bye to my breast and gently bracing myself. There was no more to think or do. All my decisions were over for the moment. I was suspended. I inhaled the scent of Wendy's flowers and then I fell asleep, finally relaxed in the company of the unknown.

Uwe arrived at eight the next morning. He looked half asleep and frozen from the motorcycle ride. He looked worried. Others began arriving: my sister, Wendy, Ginny, and other friends. I didn't expect a crowd. I must have been very transparent—worrying over having to wait for a twelve noon surgery—and so they came.

A nurse insisted I take a Valium pill, and within twenty minutes I was hosting a party from a hospital bed at ten in the morning. I had planned a soulful farewell to my breast. But with this audience and the Valium, it became a shocking entertainment with me as the star. I pulled the hospital gown off and draped my secondhand red satin robe behind me, ever mindful of the color film in Uwe's camera and the otherwise sterile color scheme of the hospital room. Then Wendy selected stems from her exotic bouquet and arranged them ceremoniously about my exposed breasts. Odalisque in a hospital bed. Uwe began taking pictures. But the farewell-to-my-breast photo session ended with the arrival of another nurse.

"They'll be coming for you soon," she said and gave me an

injection of morphine. I said "Ouch" very loudly. There was something about the rushed manner of the nurse that frightened me.

On the heels of the morphine, the gurney arrived. Seeing the orderly wheel the gurney toward me was the closest thing to seeing my coffin arrive. I insisted that I climb onto it, rather than be hoisted from my bed. I lay down on the gurney. They covered me tightly in a sheet, like a corpse in a shroud. Once we took off, I got a flat-on-my-back tour of the hospital ceilings. It was a new view of the world.

Uwe and Wendy followed alongside, while Gale stayed behind. I kept them in view and held Uwe's hand. And I had to laugh. The orderly dumped his Filipino newspaper on the pristine sheet on top of my presurgical pristine body. There can only be so much control, even in a hospital. Then we entered a cargo elevator. In hospitals the cargo is often operating-room patients. The walls were padded with packing blankets to protect the elevator from me and my fellow traveler in the elevator that day, an aluminum stacking box for hot lunches.

"You can't go any farther," the orderly told my friends. I looked up at them with scared eyes. We kissed good-bye. This was it then. They make you go into the operating room alone.

The large double doors to the pre-op room swung open like the doors of a restaurant kitchen, and they wheeled me through. It reminded me of the entrance to Steeplechase, the old Coney Island amusement park ride where you entered through the double doors of a guy's smile and got ten rides for a dollar.

"Linda, Linda. Do you know where you are?" strange people dressed in green gowns and shower caps asked me.

"Yes," I said, not really sure. I remembered my name.

"Good news, Linda. Your breast is still on! They couldn't confirm malignancy." The words rattled in my skull, like the sound of a bowling ball hitting wooden pins. I couldn't count how many pins were left standing. I hadn't understood. What was my score?

"We could not confirm malignancy in the frozen section taken from your breast. So far, we've done a kind of lumpectomy, until we get further analysis of the tissue. It's very good news, but we don't know exactly what it means yet."

I went back to sleep.

When they swung me out of the cargo elevator back toward my room, I saw Ruth, the breast-screening nurse who had discovered my lump two weeks before.

"Ruth, did you hear the news? My breast is still on!" I screamed to her, still prostrate on the gurney.

Ruth looked astonished. It wasn't what I was saying but that I was saying anything at all. She couldn't believe I was hawking her like a sideshow barker as I was being wheeled back from the operating room.

The next morning, I was mildly feisty. I wanted the intravenous tube out and I wanted to eat. I was trying to build my courage back up, wondering if it was safe to hope. Would there be no mastectomy after all? I was utterly confused by this turnabout. Within twenty-four hours I found myself at home alone with my sixteen bouquets and twelve boxes of Pepperidge Farm cookies and other offerings of a day's worth of visitors. Then, the telephone rang.

"The good news is that the cancer has not invaded," Dr. Elliot reported. "You have in-situ carcinoma. But . . . but the cancer extends to the margin in twenty out of twenty-four pathology slides. In other words, it's larger than what we took out—very large indeed—and I think you still need to go back for the mastectomy."

I took three weeks to think it over. I saw an army of doctors to get their opinions. It was difficult to reconcile that while my prognosis had dramatically improved, my treatment options had not. The cancer was contained in the milk ducts of my breast. Given the size and density (meaning it was difficult to obtain easy-to-read mammograms) of my breast, the only sure way to prevent the prospect of invasive cancer was with mastectomy. It seemed as if my breast was too large and too dense to preserve and safely monitor.

I decided to stay with Dr. Elliot. He was an excellent doctor at one of the best teaching hospitals in the country. He was a straight talker and answered all my questions. He was the one who first told me I was ill. He was the one whose eyes I looked into before losing consciousness in the operating room the first time around. And on top of that, I appreciated his fascination for medicine, a fascination I shared, even though this case was my own. Dramatic events had forged our doctor-patient relationship. I had already crossed the Antarctic with Dr. Elliot so, to me, our bond was unbreakable. Changing doctors now would have been like exchanging the groom for the best man in the middle of a wedding ceremony.

The choice was excruciating. I could give up my breast or have it cut away gradually until the pathology slides confirmed that they had got it all—for now. And try as I might, I couldn't forget my recent frantic bargains with God, when I promised *anything* in order to survive. A month later, my breast came off.

3

When it was time to get undressed I had to whip myself into action. At first I couldn't bring myself to look down at my mastectomy scar, let alone gaze at it in a mirror. The view just beyond my nose was almost too close. I would have been perfectly happy to spend the rest of my life with blinders on, because facing the mirror was the first and most basic step that I took toward facing myself, literally and figuratively. And that first look, post-mastectomy, was a shocking view of the change at its worst.

It was another full week before I could shower. The smell of the hospital was still on me. It was perversely comforting but also a sign of my vulnerability. At last, I was willing and anxious to wash it away. My mother stood by to help me. Her face was tense as she watched me undress. The closer I came to unveiling myself to her for the first time, the more her mouth tightened. Then it relaxed.

The scar was red and straight and it crossed the upper half of a slight adolescent mound. This was my post-mastectomy consolation prize, a rudimentary beginning to reconstruction. A total of 200 cc's of saline solution were pumped into the reconstructive device in my chest at the time of surgery.

I let the shower spray run on "that side" and lightly washed "there." At first I washed with the soap in my hand. That way I had a barrier between my hand and the strange feeling of my almost flat and nippleless skin with its hot water bottle of an expandable temporary reconstructive device beneath it. I let the strip bandages—which surgeons use to hold things together—stick on my chest way too long. I let them disintegrate over time, slumped like old banana skins across my chest until they were washed away in the shower. When I finally washed myself directly, I was as skittish as if I was trying to wash a stranger.

My mother stayed on for three weeks in my apartment designed for one. She slept in the living room on the fold-out couch and I slept on a futon in the dining room. In the mornings, I would get out of my bed and move to the couch for a nap. I couldn't understand why I was so tired, or how it was that my mother arrived home first when we went out on a short walk for the first time. A few days later, to prove myself, I actually walked four miles, to the Golden Gate Bridge and back, despite my mother's protests. Then I slept for the next two. Meanwhile, my mother hauled groceries and laundry up Nob Hill and three flights of stairs. Sometimes she joined me for a rest in the sun.

I arranged for a visit from a Reach to Recovery volunteer during that first week at home. I had questions about the recovery process, about reconstruction, and about sex. I made it clear that I wanted a volunteer close to my own age. Then I made it clear to my mother that I wanted her to leave while we talked.

"Why?" she asked me.

"There's no privacy here. I want to talk to her alone," I said. I wasn't able to tell my mother that I wanted to talk to this stranger about sex and mastectomy. Perhaps I couldn't tell my mother because my mother had never really talked to me about sex. In fact, she had never really got around to menstruation either. It was Gale who handed me my first box of sanitary napkins when I was fourteen years old. After that I was totally on my own. And it was another four years before I had the courage to walk into a store and purchase what I needed.

"You want me to cook and clean for you and carry things up and down, and now you dismiss me? I'm not the maid. I'll sit here quietly. I won't listen. But I won't go."

"You have to go," I screamed.

It was three hours later, just ten minutes after the Reach to Recovery volunteer left, that my mother walked back in. "How was your visit?" she asked me.

"Where did you go?" I responded. I was feeling guilty and justified in my demands at the same time. Then I saw "Macy's" on the front of the bag. "What did you buy?"

"I bought you something more comfortable to wear," she told me, "a loose shirt that buttons down the front."

It was Uwe who drove me to the doctor in this first phase, immediately following my mastectomy. Dr. Elliot inflated the tissue expander beneath my skin with saline solution, and week by week I watched my mound grow. I was able to convince myself that the mastectomy was transitional—a mere stage in this process of what they call "immediate reconstruction." The tissue-expanding device was located under my skin, but way too far to the right, practically under my arm, so that I couldn't put my arm comfortably at my side. Yes, there was a hollow directly above it, where the soft breast tissue had been removed. Yes, the small port at my side through which the saline solution was injected seemed to jut out conspicuously. In fact, it caused much discomfort during the day. I felt like one of those teachers I had in public school—amply endowed older ladies who were always sticking their hands down their blouses to adjust the engineering.

Friends dropped by almost every night. My mother observed how, as far as men went, I seemed to divide my time between Uwe and Bill, as though these two together formed the basis of a single satisfying relationship.

My mother found Uwe fascinating and powerful, and Bill demonstrative and kind. I was indebted to both of them. Yet I knew I did not love Bill, and my feeling had only been sharpened by the cancer. In a sense he had saved my life. We stayed in close touch as friends. He brought me flowers in gold foil gift boxes, and even a book on cancer and diet, accompanied by the food required to prepare its recipes. He took me out on long drives.

Uwe called frequently too and came around a few times a week, but with the emergency over, our daily contact subsided. I missed his constant coaching, but it was no longer appropriate. I was always afraid of becoming too dependent on him. And Uwe had his own fears. As soon as the crisis and his responsibility were over, he began pulling away. I turned to other friends for the countless favors I needed as I began to regain my strength.

UP FRONT

I put aside the shifts in my support system, and the horror, the pain, the annoyances. I tried to ignore the sense of tightness and constriction, the asymmetry, and even the sight of the mastectomy scar itself, and focused on the reconstructive process. Because there is hope and expectation in this form of immediate reconstruction—as long as there is anticipation. But as the rebuilding process came to an end, my fears began to accumulate. My feelings of shock were now fully focused on my breasts, undiluted for the moment by doubts about my survival. I had only one life to live (I still wasn't quite sure if I would live it all), and the plastic surgeon was telling me that what I had left I was going to live with artificially upright, average-size breasts. Because if I wanted my two breasts to match, I would have to reduce my natural breast to the size of the soon-to-be reconstructed one. I still joked that I would be getting *Gidget Goes Hawaiian* breasts, an allusion to the once-hoped-for silhouette in the days when I was a teenager.

But reconstruction was not a cosmetic operation in the way that a very large-breasted woman might elect to remove tissue and skin and become "normal." I was a normally large-breasted woman now down to only one breast, and I was terrified. What was I to do with the one natural breast that was left to me? Would I be giving up all that I had left—sensitivity, the ability to breast-feed—in order to match a facsimile that might turn out to be no better than a wooden leg?

I had felt confined by my Bali three-hook underwire support system from the time I was a teenager, and suddenly three hooks were no longer a necessity. But it is not easy to replace a body image that one has nurtured since adolescence, since those summers when I hung out with the kids on Eighty-sixth Street in Brooklyn. A guy called Beans LaBrutzi once told me

I looked like Sophia Loren when the two of us were leaning against a parked car. From then on, it did not matter if I gained weight or lost weight. It did not matter that the exquisite structure of Ms. Loren's face was entirely different from my own or that my nose was twice the size of hers. I saw myself as the full-bodied, earthy, sexy, sultry, passionate woman she often played in the movies. And anyway, she and I both had brown hair.

With my mastectomy my body image suffered a head-on collision, and emotionally I *was* like a teenager again. I was young enough and single enough that my whole emotional future seemed connected to how my body looked. So you can imagine my feelings three months later when I returned to the hospital to complete my reconstruction. As I walked back through the pre-operating room doors, I remembered that they had seemed like the teeth of death when they wheeled me in, Valiumed and morphined, for mastectomy surgery. Now I faced the final phase of reconstruction, a three-hour operation upon which I imagined my identity would rest.

I was shown to a curtained cubicle and told to undress. A nurse gave me a garment bag which, when filled with my sweater and coat, looked oddly reminiscent of the gray body bags on the evening news. Dressed once again in my hospital gown, I felt like a prisoner waiting for my sentence to be carried out. I alternated between reliving the horrors of my mastectomy and anticipating my reconstruction, the great consolation fantasy I clung to so as not to fully experience the loss of my breast.

When I awoke I felt as if my breasts were thumbtacked bolt upright to the recovery room ceiling. The doctors—a team of nameless residents who assisted at the plastic surgery operation—came by to tell me it went well. "You should be pleased." Then they explained that my natural breast was set much higher because in time gravity would pull it down. Also, the nipple was farther down because when the breast dropped the nipple would eventually move into place. And this was my healthy breast! Of my reconstructed breast, they reported that it was placed lower because in time it would migrate upward. Then they told me, almost as an aside, that yet *another* incision, in the shape of a Z, had been made. It dovetailed nicely with the mastectomy scar, they thought. This was necessary, they said, to get the right angle of "projection." Oh, and the nipple was still missing, of course. That would come later. Of course.

My God, I thought. My breasts are a mess.

I expected Marcia to call from England when I was at the hospital, but she didn't. It was almost a week later, when I was recuperating at Gale's, that she finally called.

"How come I haven't heard from you? Where have you been?" I asked.

"I would have called you sooner, but I've been in hospital myself, Linda."

"You have? Why?"

"I have breast cancer."

What Marcia discovered was a pea-size lump at twelve o'clock on her right breast, at exactly the same location that cancer was discovered in mine. The mammogram showed nothing, but Marcia had the lump biopsied anyway. It was positive. "Empathy is a part of my profession," Marcia told me, "but this is ridiculous."

We discussed treatment options and argued over the differences in approach between English and American medicine. The English, I found out, do not routinely sample the lymph nodes as a way of staging the disease. But Marcia had done her research. Her cancer was invasive, but it was very early. She felt confident with lumpectomy and radiation.

The discovery of cancer in my sister's breast was devastating news to me. I was worried about her and now I had new worries about myself. I knew that there was additional risk for an occurrence in what was left of my remaining breast. Marcia, my mother, and Gale were all at increased risk too. Frightening as these facts were to both Marcia and me, there was also something in our shared illness that was comforting, albeit strange. It had eliminated the nagging early guilt, the question of "Why me? What did I do wrong to cause this?" Because even though there was no known family history preceding us, there was now the unarguable certainty of some familial predisposition that had affected us both.

I brooded over Marcia's illness as I recovered from the reconstructive surgery. In my Hollywood version, the patient would be miraculously transformed without scars, swelling, or bruises. But in real life I knew it wouldn't be that simple. What I didn't know was how complicated it would be. Because what I really faced wasn't so much the sight of my physical reconstruction but the process of emotional reconstruction that had begun with mastectomy and that would continue for months—and years—to come.

Although I probably would have denied it, I sought this operation with the vague hope that my physical and psychological transformation would be complete through the medical manipulation of skin, muscle, and implant. But that was not possible. At best, when I woke up after reconstruction, I felt married to a stranger. And it was not merely occupying my bed; it was permanently embedded in my body! Reconstruction was not the whole solution. The basic task remained the same as it had been at the time of my mastectomy three months before. I still had to rebuild my psychological self-image. Reconstruction just gave me a little bit more to work with.

It was my own advance fantasies that had turned reconstruction into a miracle cure. The doctors had told me that my breasts would drop and rise, but I wasn't prepared for breasts that were two different sizes, one projecting out naturally, like a teardrop, while the other was no better than a flattened nippleless mound of dirt sitting on my chest wall. And then to add insult to injury, they instructed me to massage the damn thing for half an hour in the morning and again at night, because it was hard. Hard. It was rocklike! And even on my natural breast, the incisions began to tighten and stiffen like a rope holding my breast to my body.

So instead of the moment of transformation I had hoped for, reconstruction left me poised in a love/hate relationship with my body, a delicate balance that fluctuated as wildly as my female hormones in anticipation of the onset of menstruation. I resented the potential problems with the implant—the hardening—even if it was a natural part of the healing process. I wanted the implant to stop being "false" and simply become a part of me. I wanted and expected that reconstruction would be "done to me" and that I would have no work or responsibility in the matter. My breasts had required no attention from me before. And that's the way I wanted them to be again. I wanted no reminders of the change, no reminders of what I had been through. But each step in the process became just that: a little dash of salt in the wound to remind me. And only after a lot of pain did I eventually come to accept the change.

Acceptance is not a simple state. It evolves. And it includes crying over the unjustness of mastectomy itself or what they call reconstruction. No amount of massaging was going to remove the Z that now adorned the side of my fake mound. The top of the Z linked up with the big "dash" of the mastectomy scar that ran along the front of my chest. My only consolation, arrived at after weeks of searching, was that the isometric exercise involved in pushing my breast around seemed to be keeping my upper arms in pretty good condition. And with time, the massage became routine. I worked at it during reruns of *Barney Miller*, or late-night telephone conversations with friends.

Then one day a moment came in this "dance" with myself when I realized that maybe I could fall back in love with myself again. For me, massaging my reconstructed breast for months and months after reconstruction was the first stage in a kind of bonding with my new body. I got to know the boundaries of sensitivity on my chest wall and the areas of numb woodenness. I also got to know the strength and durability of the implant, since as my frustration mounted, my gentleness waned. The exercise of rubbing got to be a daily conversation with my breast—in the early days hostile and then later, resigned. Finally we were like an old married couple, so in sync that we no longer had to talk. And from that state flowed memories and ideas: recollections of bikinis in the back of the closet, the idea of hugging, even of showing myself off. Although I didn't recognize them as such, these were the first steps in rebuilding my self-image. And as the ideas poured out I tried them on, literally and figuratively. I tried them on for myself first and then for friends and eventually even for strangers— strangers who were men.

During one of my massage sessions, I remembered that I still had an old tiny red bikini that I bought in Mexico. It had made me feel like a salami in the skin of a frankfurter—oozing out of both ends. I decided to try it on for the first time in years.

To my amazement, my breasts were now very decently covered. It was a stroke of good fortune that the style perfectly suited my new topography—a straight band of material that miraculously covered every ugly red scar. Even better, I noticed that my breasts were self-supporting enough so that they sat nicely within the skimpy pockets without the bra strings digging into the back of my neck.

It was my first opportunity to see—to my surprise and pleasure—that my body could again be appealing. It was a significant moment. For the first time since my diagnosis, I saw the possibility of feeling sexy. That I could be attractive when covered so skimpily opened up the possibility that I could also look good when totally uncovered and exposed. And it was only from this perspective, at this first moment of satisfaction with myself, that I could stand back and once again get a glimmer of my own worth—with or without my breast.

But there are also women like Catherine, a divorced woman of forty-five, who told me flatly, "I like my body much better now, since the surgery." Catherine was not going to have reconstruction so she could fit somebody's mold of how she should look. Period.

Yet, reconstruction was a necessary follow-up to mastectomy for *me*. No doubt I had been too much influenced by advertising about the importance of physical beauty. But in my experience, we are best able to evaluate the worth of things from a position of having. And from that moment with my bathing suit on, it was as though I had gotten two breasts back. It was only after I got them back that I began to determine if breasts were what was essential or not in my feeling emotionally whole.

A few days later, I passed a one-armed man on the street. I glanced at his stub and kept walking. The experience was disturbing. I had the faint wish—barely conscious—that I didn't have to see such a thing. It was as though a small voice inside me said, "Why do you have to show that to me? You are making me uncomfortable."

But the image of that man stayed with me. Unconsciously I knew a time would come when some form of testing and exposure—and hopefully acceptance—would also be necessary for me.

Eventually, I was willing to risk a little. My first step was to organize a dinner for a group of women friends. After we ate, I simply announced that I wanted to try on my bikini and show them how it looked. A strange after-dinner activity, but not for a post-mastectomy woman. And my friends understood. They seemed pleased that I was asking them to participate and encouraged me like cheerleaders. When I walked out of the bathroom into the softly lit living room, I was greeted with oohs and aaahs. A teenager in her first prom dress. Sort of.

My friends assured me that I looked fantastic. I pointed out all the imperfections to them. They argued with me and impressed upon me that no one has a perfect body.

Buoyed by their reactions, and probably by the wine I had had with dinner, I decided to have my *real* questions answered and my *real* body image tested. I removed my top and showed them the state of things at one month post-reconstruction. I don't know and will never know for sure what they thought or what they felt in their hearts or stomachs. Perhaps they silently thanked their lucky stars that it wasn't them. But I prefer to believe what they told me. They were amazed at how good it looked. The mere idea that the implant was contained beneath my own skin and was therefore a part of my body startled and impressed them.

My friends assured me that there was nothing about it that would horrify anyone, including a lover. And for that reason alone there is real value in exposing oneself within the safe environment of one's friends.

As a result, I came away with new words with which to describe my altered body in my own mind. My friends said I was still "two-breasted." It replaced "mutilated," "chopped off," and "ugly." I began to accept the notion that I was different as a result of surgery, but that everybody is somewhat different and that the difference was not as negative and devastating as it first seemed.

And ultimately every woman who has had a mastectomy must do the same. She must in her own way expose herself to achieve a level of psychological comfort and acceptance. Because in time, when I looked at myself every morning in the mirror, I was more able to say, "Well, that's just me there," instead of "Oh yes, I'm ugly."

But having broken through that huge first barrier, I realized something else—I didn't like to hug. The sensation was new and strange. All I could think about was the contrast with how my reconstructed side felt and my memory of a real, complete hug. And I automatically assumed that the strange sensation, the dull pressure of the implant against my ribs, felt just as odd and obvious to the other person as it did to me. I became unwilling to hug.

After a few weeks, I brought up my fears with my therapist, Sam. The solution was obvious. He offered to hug me. "It feels soft and symmetrical," he told me. His comment was a revelation. I suddenly understood the distinction between what I was feeling and the experience of the person who was pressing against me.

Still, my confidence faltered. So I tried the experiment myself. I took my own index fingers and from the "outside," with my fingers pointing at my breasts, I poked each of them with my eyes closed. They felt almost identical. The reconstructed side was somewhat firmer, but I decided that it was flexible and soft enough to seem natural to anyone else.

So a hug was not a dead giveaway. I accepted that it felt okay to other people. At last I had regained confidence and comfort in at least one innocent physical expression of affection. Because without that basic gesture how could I ever hope to use my body in more sexual ways?

Yet my fears rose in direct proportion to my optimism. Hopefulness gave rise to risk-taking, and the risks, no matter how small, frightened me to death. My short-term goal was to test my self-image in tiny but reassuring ways as a prelude to some unknown moment in the future.

Even in the wake of mastectomy and an incomplete and imperfect reconstruction, my sexuality began to stir. I started to walk around naked at home in order to feel myself again as a sexual being. I needed to consciously feel my body moving through space. It was a gentle warm-up for the future, for that still-unspecified time when I might be naked in front of a man.

I felt ready to take another, much bolder step. I called Bill, the man who had urged me to get my breasts checked in the first place. I asked him to give me a massage.

Suddenly the need to be touched soothingly, to reestablish contact between my bare skin and a pair of bare hands that were not my own, had become urgent. It wasn't until I was on my way to his house that it dawned on me that in order to have my back massaged, I might also have to expose my front.

I couldn't imagine revealing myself to a stranger yet, but I felt ready to tackle Bill, a man whom I knew, whom I trusted, who had seen me naked before and, most importantly, one for whom I harbored no emotional longings or sexual fantasies whatsoever. I also knew that Bill's mother had had a mastectomy.

Bill made every sign of casually expecting me to undress in front of him. My reaction startled me: I didn't care. If anything, I almost welcomed the opportunity. If there is a scale for such things, my anxiety was only a few notches above undressing in front of my women friends. Somehow being exposed in front of Bill seemed safe, because the context was absolutely nonsexual and more in the realm of research for me.

"What do you think?" I asked.

"Obviously, it's not your real breast," he said.

Was he repulsed by what he saw? I strained to see if there was even a hint of distaste on his face. None. Bill went on, "The main thing is that your nipple is missing. How come the scar is so high up?"

I explained that it had to do with the location of the tumor. "All in all, it's not bad," he pronounced. But he had said so little I was dissatisfied. I wanted to hear that it was great or horrible, some kind of dramatic response, although hopefully one closer to what I had gotten from my women friends.

Instead, Bill downplayed the situation. He tried to make me understand that it was not that important. Ironically, he seemed to understand the situation better than I did. As he said, "If any guy expected you to conform to a *Playboy* pinup, then he isn't anyone you want to know anyway."

The problem, though, wasn't so much with "any guy" but with myself. What I learned from that brief encounter was that a part of me still expected to conform, not necessarily to *Play-*

boy, but to some classic feminine image. And realizing this, I knew that I would have to begin to give up—or at least redefine—my idea of what feminine was. But I had no idea how to begin.

At the heart of my struggle was the need to be "whole" despite the reality of what I had become. My former self—as imperfect as I knew myself to be—was like a standard of lost perfection. That is why, in that first moment before the mirror, I did not look at myself. I did not know what to expect. Then, I simply did not *want* to know. Now I was caught in the sometimes slow process of getting to know through that part of day-to-day living that is never a fully realized state, but a truce, a constant negotiation with reality. How, in that state, was I to create a sense of physical and emotional well-being in a world inhabited by seemingly perfect men and women? I had made some progress, but I was taking only tiny steps forward and it all seemed so slow.

4

"How are you?" a stranger asks.

How indeed?

"Cancer has consumed my life and thoughts for months," I want to say. "They have hacked my breast off. Can you tell?"

I felt ready to hurl myself at all the risks waiting to be taken. Except one. Because having experienced even the shock of cancer—my new yardstick for lesser fears and doubts—I seemed to be living life like a nervous poker player only when it came to the subject of men.

I believed they couldn't or wouldn't want me. And such fears dogged my reality as well as my dreams. I clung to a long list of familiar former lovers, one-time boyfriends such as Uwe. I clung to them because no matter how painful the breakups had been, at least they had known me before that moment of destruction to my body. It was the new men that I feared.

I attended my first post-mastectomy art opening haunted by these feelings. There was a handful of people, men and women, I could have said hello to. But I hid. I took my feelings of inadequacy, my fears about having to expose myself, and turned them inside out. I decided that I didn't want to talk to anyone. I flitted around the gallery, looked at the floor, and avoided all contact. I didn't even look up at the paintings. I roamed around with my pain, and when it became unbearable, I left.

A week later at a reception at work, an attractive artist struck up a conversation with me. To my surprise, I was pleased by his attention. I had been curious about Robert when he showed up at the Exploratorium as an artist-in-residence, well before I had been diagnosed with breast cancer. But little more than one month after my mastectomy, I wasn't interested in this man for himself. I was only curious about his species in general and I desperately wanted to know only one thing: how I looked to him.

He looked me straight in the face. His eyes felt like the first pair of eyes that I had ever been confronted with. I felt stripped and transparent. Perhaps he had heard about my illness and was approaching me out of a macabre interest. There could be no other reason.

"How are you?" he said, as though we talked often. He rambled on, revealing facts about himself that were clearly designed to impress me. He let me know that he was divorced by mentioning his kids and *their* mother.

"What about you?" he asked.

I was caught. I was talking to a man whom I found attractive and who made no secret of being interested in me. I did not like him for those very reasons. His aggressiveness seemed to confirm that he ran after all women. Why else would he be talking to me? I was certain that he knew about my mastectomy and that I was a curiosity. I hated him although I was fascinated by his method of "chatting me up." It seemed like a method to me because I was overly conscious of what he was saying, too aware of my own situation—it was no longer conversation but the beginning of strategic warfare. And there was only one way for me to win.

"I don't know if you've noticed, but I've been away for a month," I said.

"Why?" A fair question and one I set him up for.

"I had breast cancer and had my breast removed," I said, point-blank. "And I don't yet know how it will affect my life as a single woman."

He stood there. "You mean you haven't been with anyone yet?"

"No, not yet."

"Well, you look fine to me," he said. The message was implicit. "Let's sit down and talk some more."

"I have to leave now," I said. I didn't wait for him to respond. I turned my back and ran. I couldn't look at him again. I had blurted out devastating news to a virtual stranger. I did it to drive him away and, damn him, it didn't work. When he wouldn't leave, I had to. I was caught between my desire for attention and my obvious inability to accept it.

I ran into Robert in the offices of the Exploratorium weeks later. My stomach sank when I saw him. He asked how I was and I said "Fine," without looking up from my shoes. I made it clear that there was nothing further to say.

A few weeks later, I was invited to another party. I rarely attended so many social events, but I was making a huge effort to get back into the world.

Many of the guests were single, and I found myself surrounded by both men and women I had never met before. I started talking with an architect, Eric. I was not in the least attracted to Eric, so I consented to talk to him, congratulating myself on my willingness to carry on a conversation. I thought of it as a step forward, a vast improvement over my behavior with Robert. I was there, eating and talking with friendly people. I was out among my peers. I made no mention of cancer. There was no obvious difference between us.

In the course of our conversation Eric told me he moved to San Francisco after his mother's illness and death. I tried to dismiss my desire to know, but finally I asked, "What did she die of?"

"Breast cancer," he said.

Why would anyone, let alone a guy whose mother died of breast cancer, want to get to know someone like me? I asked myself. It was as though I had forgotten that Bill, the very man who had urged me to have my breasts checked, had a mother who underwent mastectomy. I was the one who couldn't or wouldn't accept Bill. And now I was about to do the same to Eric. I blurted out the news.

"I've had breast cancer and a mastectomy," I said.

What can anyone say, especially if you are total strangers engaged in otherwise polite conversation. I instantly felt ridiculous.

Eric said good-bye to me at the end of the evening—good-bye, with no attempt at further contact. I felt sad. And I actually believed that he had rejected me because of my cancer and my loss of a breast.

UP FRONT

Three months after my mastectomy and one week before reconstructive surgery, I decided to fly to the East Coast. The mere fact that I was on a plane and going somewhere—not interviewing doctors, not listening to their muffled whispers behind closed doors, not languishing on examination tables in backless cotton gowns or waiting in corridors—made me expect a made-for-TV movie romance would unfold immediately. Who would the man in the next seat be?

Naturally, "he" was a young and mercifully unfriendly woman. So I immediately changed my seat and stretched out across an empty row in the center section. I slept like the heroine in a fairy tale, waiting for the real world to begin. When I woke up I was in Newark. Not exactly the backdrop for a fantasy.

From behind my very California mirrored sunglasses I watched people in line for the bus into Manhattan. I stood with one hand on my hip in my bulky V-neck sweater and jeans. I tested my secret. Could I wait there with my temporary internal prosthesis, a big unwieldy orb under my skin, and still look good?

The answer was yes.

In New York City the answer from men on the street is always yes. I was still in New Jersey. But I drank up those yeses. I carved notches in my belt by the second, deliriously feeling my attractiveness in the crowds of people—mysterious, inviting, and threatening. I was intimidated but I felt alive.

As I stood there, I looked right into the eyes of a man as he walked past carrying his luggage and odd paraphernalia in open shopping bags. He stared right back at me and then he stopped farther up, also waiting for the bus. True, I was wearing my sunglasses but I felt very bold. I suddenly felt a rush of adrenaline. In that instant of contact, I became a little like a crazy person, impervious to the constraints of normal citizens. I had no fear. I had faced cancer. My desire for contact was suddenly stronger than reason.

I picked up my bag and walked closer. I stopped right alongside him, waited a moment, and then came out with a ridiculous question.

"I just have to ask you," I said, "what's that in your shopping bag?" It looked like a long ruler with strings attached to it. The tension was electric. I was hell-bent on electrocuting myself in the humid air.

"It's an architectural tool. I'm an architect." I found out that his name was Sean, that he was a native Californian living in New York.

"No kidding. I'm a native New Yorker living in California," I said.

It got to be a little like a Woody Allen movie. We talked about the difference in the quality of the light in New York and California and the people on either coast, the pristine existence of a boy growing up in Westwood and the gritty street games of a girl playing in Brooklyn.

By the time the bus had pulled in, I was helping him carry his shopping bag with its giant ruler on board. We sat together.

The sun was setting as we crept into New York in the rush hour traffic. The sky across the Hudson River and Manhattan was orange and pink. In the midst of the sunset, we were wrapped in the darkness of the bus, whispering as if we were in the same bed. Sean said, "I wish I could escort you around New York, but my girlfriend wouldn't like it."

He told me about his family and I told him about mine. Our fathers had both died early in life. He told me he had studied at Harvard and had worked with a world-famous architect. He had just quit to go into business for himself. He seemed surefooted and strong-willed.

I was frightened and uncertain, but I tried to sound convincing. All I knew for certain was that I was heading away from death. But I couldn't tell him that.

"Will you have lunch with me next week?" he asked when the bus pulled in. He walked me to Forty-second Street and outmaneuvered everyone else to hail a cab for me. He opened the taxi door and threw my bag inside. Then, in what felt like slow motion, he kissed me on the lips. "Good-bye."

The fear welled up later that night. I lay there on the foldout couch at a friend's apartment with the sounds of Manhattan shooting up into the open window on the twenty-first floor. I was trembling. With just one kiss and the promise of lunch, the made-for-TV movie had become too real.

Like some sort of debutante, I was about to formally reintroduce myself into life. I found it pretty hard not to stumble. The offer to have lunch with a man I didn't know was more than I was prepared for. My charm, my curiosity, my aggressive flirtatiousness immediately and automatically dried up.

Just as I hoped and feared, Sean called me the first thing Monday morning. "Can you still make lunch?" he asked.

I was ready with my comeback. "Come along and have lunch with my friend Kathe and me. You'll like her," I said.

Kathe was my protection, but she was running very late. So I waited for her uptown while Sean waited out of reach downtown, in front of a restaurant in Little Italy. When Kathe and I arrived at the restaurant an hour late, Sean was already gone.

I wanted to scream. Now I wasn't just fearful but frustrated. So I called Sean and asked him to meet me again. This time I waited alone outside his house. He was careful not to invite me in. We walked to a tough-guy coffee shop. We made small talk under the fluorescent lights. I felt as limp as the battered menu.

It wasn't just that Sean was a stranger. I realized I was dealing with an even greater unknown; it was, to my surprise, myself. Not two days earlier I had felt a rush of excitement when I met him; now I was just a bundle of fear and uncertainty. I braced myself with my elbows on the gold-speckled Formica table. And predictably, before the coffee had arrived, I told him that I had had cancer.

By the second cup of coffee, he had written down the names of psychology books and therapists for me to look up back in San Francisco. He wrote on a napkin in the formal and beautiful print that designers use, an upright and controlled style of writing not unlike his own carefully measured response to my story.

We left the coffee shop and strolled out along the edge of a park overlooking the Hudson River. We found a bench, and by that time I could no longer contain the desperate questions I had to ask. I asked the sorts of questions, sitting there in the park, that one asks after months of passion with a trusted lover—and then only for fun. I dispensed with even my thin veil of pride.

"Did you have any thoughts about sleeping with me?" I wanted to know. We had known each other for only two hours and yet it seemed my life depended on his answer. Because my question was serious. After thirty-four years I didn't know who I was or what impact I made. I had only a pent-up desire to test my sexuality and sensuality. But there was much fear and terror and a hundred counter-impulses to that basic motivation.

"No," he said. He put his arm around me when I started to cry. And in the end, I kissed him good-bye and said that I wanted to see him once more before I left. But I knew there would be no future meeting.

I thought about what happened with Sean often during the rest of my stay. Instead of just having a cup of coffee with this man, I was wondering where or when we were going to make love. Talk about crazy. My expectations were premature and one-sided, an unmistakable indication of my own insecurities and fears. But fearful or not, I couldn't keep any of it—not the fact of the cancer and mastectomy or my curiosity about Sean's reaction—to myself.

But there was still New York. I was on the move constantly, rushing between transplanted California friends and long-time New York ones. Even though no one in my family lived in the city anymore, I made a pilgrimage to our old house and neighborhood. My street in Bensonhurst seemed narrower and grimmer than I remembered, the houses more densely packed in; and along Twentieth Avenue, all the old candy stores I remembered were gone.

In Brooklyn, I visited Robin, a friend since junior high. She had recently separated from her husband and was attending medical school. She greeted me in the unmistakable tones of a Brooklyn accent, which, after my eleven years in California, sounded thicker than ever. First we caught up on Robin's life and then we got to mine. She knew I had breast cancer and she wanted to go over every detail of my diagnosis and treatment. Robin was more than professionally curious. She was interested and frightened because her mother had died of the disease. And she asked to see what they had done to my breasts. Then she got to her last question.

"What about guys?" Her meaning was clear.

"Well, I've learned one thing so far. I can attract them, even if what I do about it is blatant and totally botched. But

I have a hard time knowing what to do after that." I told her all about my recent encounter with Sean.

"Are you saying you felt safe flirting with him because you thought he was taken?"

"He told me he had a girlfriend," I said. "I thought it would end when we got off the bus. Up until then I felt whole and in control for the forty-five minutes it took to go from Newark to downtown Manhattan."

"He threw a wrench in the works by responding," Robin guessed.

"I was terrified of seeing him again. I got all discombobulated. I began flapping around that coffee shop, as insecure and sick a little chick, clutching for reassurance, as you've ever seen."

"Don't be so hard on yourself," she told me. "I don't know if I would have gotten even that far."

"But you don't know what I did! I blurted out my cancer story and with it every fear and insecurity. I talked to Sean like a diary. I gave up my dignity. I wanted to shock him. I wanted to get rid of him. I wanted him to fall in love with me instantly. I wanted his sympathy. But even his sympathy was painful. After all, I hardly knew the guy."

I was starting to learn. "This woman has had cancer" was not written across my forehead, not tattooed on my arm. And with Sean I had actually progressed from blurting the news out in the first five minutes to waiting a few hours. On the bus with him I had become as charming and provocative as I could be, all in the name of practice. I recounted the story of my life without the recent several months of cancer. I felt like a liar but I rationalized my lies of omission. Would I say to a total stranger "How do you do? I have bad breath" right off the bat?

So I reined myself in, hung on to my secret. But it felt illicit. And finally I confessed the secret of my missing breast.

When I flew home to San Francisco at the end of the week, I found a note from Sean in my mailbox, written on the inside of an old Christmas card.

"I really do want you to know that I am really glad we met. I am especially glad that you told me so much about yourself— it is for me one of life's joys to be with someone who can and will talk about herself, as you did. I made a mistake in not simply introducing you to my girlfriend as a friend I had met on the bus. I want you to know that I think about you—and that I know that this is a very very difficult time for you. Be smart. Be brave (but not too brave). Be well fast. I will be thinking of you. Sean."

Looking back, I see that all that happened was that a strange man asked me to lunch. He was somehow intrigued and wanted to get together again. That was all. But I didn't know how to integrate this chance meeting with the life-threatening experience of cancer. From my perspective as a post-mastectomy woman, I immediately saw such interest in sexual terms, and an internal alarm went off.

"Who am I? What do I have left to offer? Who would want me?" I asked myself. Because of one scratch on the veneer, my finish fell off.

I was coming face-to-face with the emotional aftermath of mastectomy.

5

The headline read REDFORD SEEKS STREISAND and went on from there. "Academic, 39, 6', 175 lbs, blue eyes, light brown hair, highly educated, attractive, sensual and sensitive man, seeks deep-eyed, dark-haired, smart, attractive woman for a cup of coffee and maybe *The Way We Were*." I immediately understood the implication of the ad. The advertiser, although a WASP like Redford, was hopelessly drawn to women like me. So I did an outrageous thing for me, one which illustrates the small unexpected changes that accompany a standoff with a life-threatening disease. I answered that personal ad.

It was almost four months after my mastectomy and two weeks after my final reconstruction. I had reached a momentary truce with myself. I had begun to adjust to my body and was learning how to keep my secret. My sense of self was changing daily, but I was no longer able to watch and wait. I wanted to focus on the future instead of the past, to stop dreaming about imaginary lovers and to turn in the direction of a new one. Well, kind of.

But first I made one futile attempt to take the simple way out. Ben, an old friend, was in town from Montana. He was tall, burly, benign, and fond of me, and I determined that this would be an excellent opportunity to try out my new sexual self. But Ben stubbornly and wisely would not comply with my wishes, despite the fact that a part of his trip was specifically to see me.

"Is it because I had a mastectomy?" I shrieked, confronting him with my paranoid suspicions.

"The fact that you've lost your breast makes no difference in my feelings toward you," he said. "I simply do not want to place my emotions at the mercy of your changeable needs and whims."

I wanted to learn that my body was still beautiful and workable, albeit changed, and that I could be a desirable sexual partner. Ben had told me as much in words, but now words were not enough for me. Since I was going to have to risk rejection as part of the process of my emotional healing, I knew nothing could save me from the fearful prospect of having to meet a new man.

So I answered the ad. With pen and ink I composed a letter, describing myself in these words: "5' 6", 135 lbs," "smart," "attractive," "quick-witted," "sharp-tongued," and "strong-featured." I wrote the simple facts, but they rang in my ears like lies. Because with each word, I thought about the part I was leaving out.

Unbelievably, I got a response! It was arranged that "Redford" was to call me at work the next day and I would slip away to meet him over coffee.

All day I was barely able to concentrate. As the workday wore on, I noticed that the pressure intensified and, with it, the impossibility of the rendezvous. By lunchtime he hadn't called. Instead of disappointment, I felt relief. Then the telephone rang.

I thought twice about answering it. If it was him, I would have to tell him that it was too late now and that I was too busy and that it would just have to be some other time.

I picked up the phone.

"A Tom is here to see you," the receptionist announced. "Here?"

I stiffened. How dare he come without calling first as we had agreed? I was already out of my office door. I felt nothing but anger, not nervousness or curiosity or fear.

I spied a man looking at one of the exhibits in the emptiness of the closed museum. I called his name. "Tom?" He turned toward me.

I launched into my cold little speech. "You should have called first. You are late and things have gotten out of control and I'm just too busy to leave."

He offered his excuses. But it was only after I had spoken and cut off all possibility of a meeting that I finally took the time to notice the man before me.

Tom had a small nose and high cheekbones, the classically northern European chiseled features of a distant cousin of Robert Redford. It was like that scene from *Annie Hall* where two prospective lovers meet and exchange meaningless dialogue while subtitles come up on the screen and reveal what they are really thinking. "He's not that bad" flashed across my mind.

He had taken me at my word and was about to leave. "I'll walk you to the door," I quickly intervened. We walked out into the bright sunlight of the afternoon and stood beneath the arched portico of the museum.

"So why did you run this ad?" I asked, posing the most leading question I could muster. The answer took a good ten minutes.

"Are you sure you can't slip away for some coffee?" he asked. After all, I was still standing there.

"Absolutely not," I countered, even as I remained outside talking, shifting from foot to foot and avoiding the subject of cancer. There is much to find out about a stranger, and I danced around his more difficult questions to me, mainly by asking the hard ones myself.

I struggled to keep myself there, to let our acquaintance get a toehold. How odd that I had willfully arranged the meeting and that a part of me now wanted to flee. But I held on, balancing at the edge of a psychological precipice. I suspended my fear and judgment and persisted for an hour.

I was ambivalent all right, and my ambivalence was even mirrored in the way I was dressed. I wore a fitted turquoise shirt, with a wide-cut neck that would often slip low off one shoulder, and tight pants. But it was all disguised by an oversized man's sweater that stretched from shoulder to mid-thigh.

My sense of self seemed to come and go with unpredictable rapidity. But it was looking Tom in the eye that did it. I saw an opportunity there. I realized that that was all I was seeking. With such a manageable goal, I was able to persist. I let myself explore. I kept talking. He kept talking. And for the moment,

I guarded beneath my bulky sweater the secret I might have to reveal in the future.

We set up a real date—a hike—for the following week. I showed up in a T-shirt and sweater—and shorts. Lots of people hike in shorts and boots. But my legs have always been an embarrassing feature in my self-image. I considered my legs to be thick tree stumps until I noticed that the bulky boots set them off to good advantage. So I wore boots even though they weren't necessary for the mild terrain. I took along my jeans, too, lest at the last minute my courage fail. I was striving to look attractive, even sexy, when my breasts were no longer an attraction.

I was to pick Tom up at the foot of Nob Hill. I stopped my car for the first person I saw wearing a backpack on the appointed corner. He looked only vaguely familiar through the windshield, but luckily it was him. It was probably another hour before I looked at him directly. I was too nervous.

The idea of a hike in the country suited my tentative feelings about a first date. It is an activity that can be both solitary and shared. We walked single file along narrow paths and inclines. We continued to talk, but the physical separation and the inability to look into the face of the other person kept me comfortably at a distance.

Where the path widened, I focused more closely on Tom and his stories and the observations that he made. I made an effort to get to know him, and to let him know me. But when it seemed too hard or the questions touched on dangerous ground, I retreated to vague answers and the sight of open fields around me.

Finally Tom suggested that we sit, eat, and talk. "Look over there," he said, "at that hawk," and he touched my shoulder to get me to look up. I was stunned. It wasn't a sexual touch.

But I was shocked at that moment of first contact. It made my whole body vibrate with the need for physical comfort and reassurance. I nonchalantly looked up at the hawk. But all I could see was that we were sitting close together on an open cliff overlooking the ocean, with the fog just beginning to envelop us in its hazy softness. I never once looked at Tom by my side. As we talked, I stared outward at the water.

It turned out to be a safe, conversation-based date, and for the most part I felt comfortable. But there were moments of extreme awkwardness. If he only knew what was really going on beneath my sweater, I thought. My impulse was to blurt out all the discomfort I felt but I kept it under control. There would be ample time to reveal myself.

It is no accident that I found Tom, my first post-mastectomy date, through an ad. Because as the details of this first date suggest, I wanted to "come out" and to hide at the same time.

With a letter and a postage stamp, I had thrust myself into another world. I had entered the life of a person whom I did not know and who didn't know me. I liked the fact that Tom and I had absolutely no context for each other except for the one we might create. I suppose I felt anonymous and protected.

It's not that I actively sought to segregate Tom from the rest of my life. I reported to my women friends and family about our date, just as I had told them about Sean in New York. But, I took this and each subsequent tentative step in private, reporting back to my friends only after the fact because I was afraid I might lose heart or fail.

I was trying to handle it on my own because, from as far back as my early childhood, I had learned to expect disappointment and didn't want others to know about it. I was coping very much as I had coped with menstruation, guardedly and privately and alone. I chose to date in an arena far away from the rest of my life. It didn't occur to me to ask my friends or family for help. Anyway, there was no help to be had, I felt, except perhaps through talking. I did talk to them and to my therapist, Sam, and I sulked by myself because I thought it wrong that others should see just how needy I was. Yet I also hoped they would guess. As with menstruation, I was once again embarrassed by my needs.

I was still in mourning for my breasts and for myself when I set out on my first hike with Tom. I knew I was physically strong and healthy and had bounced back well. Yet emotionally I was still a patient.

By my own design, I was feeling the greatest shock and grief at the same time as I had the least support. It's not that my friends or even my family were absent. They weren't. But I had relegated them into the background of my own personal drama. Certainly, I relied on them. There were times when, without them, I felt utterly lost. But it is also true that I felt distance as much as closeness. I saw no solution but to work my way back to wholeness alone.

I boldly scheduled my second hike with Tom ten days after the first. But just to be safe, I arranged an appointment for that evening with a friend. I wanted no temptation or possibility of lingering too long, no matter what.

My biggest problem was eye contact—it was potent stuff. Was it any wonder that I could not bring myself to look into Tom's eyes? I was afraid of what I would find there—a willing and open person looking back at me. I volunteered to drive my car again. It gave me the perfect excuse for keeping my eyes on the road, and it was a way of controlling my bouts of uncertainty.

When we finally said good-bye that day, it was in the parking lot with the sun starting to set behind us. I knew that we both had had a good time. And sure enough, Tom called me not long afterward and invited me over for the following Saturday evening.

I drove across the bridge to Tom's apartment. It was our third meeting, but when Tom answered the door I was confronted by an only vaguely familiar, somewhat pleasant-looking stranger. How could I have imagined that there might be anything between us? What had I been thinking? What was all my tension and anticipation? Who was this guy anyway?

I sat down and looked around the living room, trying to find out. There were lots of books and scholarly journals. A picture, a reproduction of a reclining nude by Modigliani, hung over the doorway that led to the bedroom. I looked at it and immediately decided that I was dealing with a man with a cultivated interest in the female form—particularly the female breast.

At dinner, intimidated by the gathering darkness and the flickering candles, I got very quiet. "I'm still not used to being around you," I said by way of explanation. Tom looked hurt.

"I can understand feeling that way the first time we met," he said, "but not now."

What I really wanted to say was "I've had a mastectomy and you don't know it and pretty soon I am going to have to tell you because the secret is weighing me down." I had a vague plan in mind—to tell him immediately before we slept together—but that prospect was still very uncertain and a long way off.

Out in the street, Tom put his arm around me when he ushered me between cars. Then our legs touched during the play we attended. And at some point, he held my hand. When we stopped at a bookstore, Tom asked me what I had been reading lately. I smiled to myself because it had been mostly cancer books. I slipped away from him and returned with a novel that I had read probably a year before. "This is one," I lied.

The touching and the questions were the small and predictable interactions between two people starting a relationship. I enjoyed them at the same time that they made me stiffen with fear. In some ways, retelling it is kind of like writing the script for a soap opera, trying to communicate the significance of every little glance, every little gesture, the lowering of the lights, the touched shoulder, the incident about the book. But the fact is that not much happened on this first date, and that's my point. Not much should happen on these early dates. At best, for a post-mastectomy woman, it is a kind of balancing act. For me it was a way of seeing how adept I had become in negotiating the fine line between self-doubt and self-confidence, between a negative body image and a gradually emerging sense of self. Or how successfully I could hold up my end of the conversation without succumbing to my deep-seated desire to expose my emotional wounds.

Each date with Tom was a trial by fire and an opportunity to reassert my self-worth. And I don't think it matters if a woman is confronting a stranger, a lover, or even a husband of many years. I have talked to many women who have walked this same high wire and, like me, they saw themselves as tightrope walkers performing a harrowing balancing act with only one breast, an umbrella, and an outstretched hand.

How can anyone feel wholly dignified when there is so much seemingly at risk? I kept up what felt like the false illusion of my wholeness. I maintained that stance for a period during which I silently drank in the looks and smiles, the attentions of this man. But it is true that I found that the effort to suppress the facts and figures of cancer required all my energy, leaving me uncertain.

Despite my slow and steady progress, I felt like a fraud. I feared Tom's rejection, imagining that sooner or later my relatively pleasing exterior would get peeled back to reveal the missing breast. Even as I passed for normal, part of me felt deformed and disfigured. I tiptoed my way around it. I didn't know or care if such self-doubt was universal. All I knew was that, as a single woman, I was taking a great risk with regard to my self-image. I saw only the risks without any assurance of positive outcomes. There is no better way to express the experience than to conjure up the uncertainty of the first dates of adolescence. The first post-mastectomy dates are a rite of passage too.

6

During three dates with Tom I had managed not to drop the bomb: the news of my mastectomy. I found Tom increasingly attractive. But each of his meaningful glances and lingering touches was like an omen in a Greek tragedy.

Late one evening, on our fourth date, after lots of talk, eye contact, touches of the hand, and spaghetti, I sat down on Tom's couch. I positioned myself in such a way that, given the coffee table right in front of me, it was impossible for Tom to sit next to me. He picked the rocker opposite. He seemed far away.

During our last hike, I had mentioned to him that I had an idea for an article. Although I never revealed its subject, it was one of many dangling clues I scattered about in the process of getting to know him. And had it not been for his sudden return to that comment, I probably would have gone home once again with my secret still under my sweater.

To my surprise and horror he said to me, "I think I know what the subject of your article will be."

"Oh?" I said.

"I think it's a health subject."

Oh God, he's figured it out, I thought. He knows! At long last the subject seemed to have introduced itself. My first feeling was one of relief.

"You're right," I said. "How did you know?"

"It's something you have or someone in your family—some condition?" he asked, and I cut him off right then. I didn't want to hear him say it, so I said it first.

"I had cancer," I said. "I've had a mastectomy."

"What—you?" he shrieked, startled and shocked. Only then did I realize that he had been expecting something along the lines of high blood pressure.

"Oh my God, I can't believe it. I can't believe that you've had cancer. You're so young," he said, and he went on like that, almost babbling, looking deeply pained and confused. He didn't know what to do, squirming in his seat and rubbing his face with his hand. "I can't believe it because I'm a breast man," he said. "I mean I have always particularly loved and appreciated women's breasts."

I looked up at the picture of the Modigliani nude. Why the hell is he telling me this? I wondered. There was nothing I could do about it now.

"What I mean to say is how tragic I think it is that doctors had to do this to you, to any woman."

Tom shifted around in his chair, in shock, alternately speechless and saying too much. I already knew that he had a phobia about doctors and hospitals because of a childhood illness. Oh perfect, I thought, when I first found out and had to laugh that my first date was with a man who had a phobia about blood and guts. Now I sat and watched its quite literal expression.

But I let him off the hook. "Don't worry if you can't take it," I said. "I've discovered that what you think or do doesn't matter to me at all." It was a discovery I made at the moment I heard myself say this; the feeling was both as strong and as transitory as my words.

As I saw him struggling, I felt stronger by the second. Watching him was like seeing my own reactions to cancer in rerun.

"I'm shocked," he said again. "And I'm uncertain. I'd hate to think I was so shallow that I would reject you because of this, but I really don't know if I can handle it." He paused. "How have other men reacted?"

I was afraid to tell him that he was my first potential lover. What if I compounded his insecurity by my own?

"I would have a hard time with this if we were still intimate," Uwe had told me when I asked him. I was crushed by his honesty. I had to remind myself that I had already found out the hard way that on a romantic level Uwe had a lot to learn.

I focused on Ben and another close male friend instead, because I liked what they both told me.

"A friend said he thought any sensitive man would naturally be nervous and afraid of his reaction and the right way to handle the situation. But others said that they thought it was no big deal," I told Tom.

With this range of responses Tom found the confidence to speak truthfully about his own doubts. "I'm afraid," he said. "But I'm also really impressed by you, by the way you're dealing with it. I've never had to actually face my own mortality. I'm sure that I would crumble if I had to confront it. You're so strong and powerful that I'm in awe."

Now he was shocking me. I sat there privately cataloging the many tiny steps of coping and preparation, as well as my fears and tears, and nothing at all about it suggested strength or valor. I had to laugh. I had always admired others for their seemingly effortless ability to know themselves and be strong. And now I was being typecast in that role. It was a wholly unexpected and marvelous turn of events, a new perspective on myself. But he was still sitting in his chair, and neither of us had moved.

At long last I saw Tom collect himself. He pulled himself together. He made a false start, trying to get up. But in the next instant, he was finally up and out of the chair, moving across the room toward me. He sat down on the edge of the coffee table in front of me and looked into my eyes and touched my cheek and said something soft. I don't remember what he said, but the gesture spoke for itself. Yet it had taken Tom one hour to cross the room to sit down beside me.

Why did I tell Tom at the moment that I did? Because I had reached the point where I felt I had to say something, even though this was not how I envisioned doing it. I planned to tell him at the time when it was apparent to both of us that we would soon become intimate. But from my behavior throughout the evening, I was beginning to see that the likelihood of our becoming close enough to sleep together was slim.

My "secret," which only a few weeks earlier helped me from saying too much too soon, had now become a barrier against getting any closer. So when the opportunity came I decided to reach out. Tom's initial reaction seemed to confirm my worst fears, but it was also a source of insight and instruction. My biggest fear had been rejection. But Tom seemed as disturbed by his own fear as he was by my news. It was then that I realized his response was more a statement about him than me. So, for the moment at least, I was only in minor danger of blaming myself.

Which is not to say that I didn't suffer. I turned my back briefly. I felt a rush of disappointment and self-pity, a glimmer of what would probably hit me once I walked out the door and drove home alone in my car. I thought, Oh God, one down and where will I find the next one and how many more will it take? Will I be able to withstand this over and over again? But I stopped myself. If there was going to be grief, I wanted it to be private.

At first, I felt hopelessly thwarted. I had come to Tom's house to experiment with my future as a woman among men. I was looking for tenderness, not a monument to my valor for facing a frightening disease. And in the end, I finally got what I had come for—the locking of eyes and a touch on the cheek—after the secret was out.

The question of whether or not I should tell was never an issue for me. But for some women the fear of rejection is so great as to convince them not to tell at all. I have spoken to women who tell about years of fully clothed sex, self-hate, and tears, all to avoid having to reveal themselves and the insecurity that comes between the moment of telling and the act of making love. For me, telling was the first word in any true emotional dialogue with Tom. It was probably the single most important factor in my emotional adjustment to mastectomy.

I certainly found myself thoroughly relaxed for the first time when I finally told Tom. The weight was off my shoulders. That lightness kindled a new level of discussion and interaction between us, softened by physical proximity and contact. And for the first time I appreciated rather than feared the opportunity to share information about myself. The weight was now on Tom's shoulders, but there was little I could do for him. I tried to let him know that I could see it there and that what happened next was up to him. If at any time he felt that it was too difficult for him to get to know me, I would accept and understand his limits, I said.

But I wasn't as passive as I perhaps sound. No longer carrying the burden, I became instantly more at home, more resourceful. I felt free for the first time to be charming and seductive. I wanted to convince Tom that I was captivating, intelligent, someone beyond a case history and a medical problem. A woman. I didn't realize that he was probably already convinced—or just about. The fact is I was convincing myself.

So I sat back against him on the couch. I sat in his arms with my legs extended and I unwound under the soft and constant movement of his hands running along my arms and in my hair. It was nothing unusual, but it felt as primal and basic as the touch of running water to a figure emerging from the desert. It seemed that for six months I had been in no one's arms, although that was not quite technically true. But to be in a new man's arms, reclining on a couch at night—that was new. And for the moment, I felt stirred, reborn, hopeful. I felt momentarily whole.

It was very late and I faced a long drive home, with the even more forbidding prospect of looking for a parking space on Nob Hill. Tom invited me to stay. "You can sleep on the couch," he said. "Or in my bed, which is very large."

"Let's eat something," I countered, like taking a line from an Ionesco play. It was an absurd response but made perfect psychological sense. I was stalling for time.

We sat and ate toast and olives in the middle of the night in Tom's kitchen, which looked as though it hadn't changed since the 1920s. I stood up on the maple dining chair in my bare feet. I sat down and extended my legs so that they rested on Tom's knees. It was three in the morning and I was feeling playful.

When Tom got up to go to the bathroom I followed him down the hall. I waited until I was left standing behind the closed door to say, "I've decided to stay. I've decided to stay with you in your bedroom if that's okay." But I set the terms. This was going to be strictly platonic, I said, and we had to wear clothes. So Tom dressed himself in a red T-shirt and jogging shorts and gave me a lovely old white cotton shirt that he had brought back from India many years before.

"I like this. Can I have it?" I joked. I put it on over my underwear.

Getting into bed is always a risk, no matter what the terms. It's not that I was afraid of being attacked or drawn into a sexual encounter. If I had felt that Tom was not trustworthy, I would never have stayed. But I had the opposite fear. I was afraid of being ignored. I could not imagine lying in bed and having absolutely no contact, not even a momentary kiss or touch as a display of affection. I was afraid of his distance. But Tom joined me on my side of the large bed. He held me and said that he was glad I stayed. "It would have been wrong for you to leave after all we have discussed," he said.

I woke up a few hours later, torn between not wanting to disturb Tom and a desire to wake him up. I solved my dilemma by going to the bathroom. But I soon discovered that I was afraid to go back to the bedroom. I had a creeping fear, something akin to the "morning after" syndrome. I felt very embarrassed. This man knew I had had cancer and only one breast and now there was daylight.

The minute I walked back into the bedroom, Tom got up

and headed straight for the bathroom. Did this mean that he wouldn't come back and would head off to the kitchen to start the day? Did he feel no desire to prolong the intimacy? Had it been established under duress? I worried over these sorts of questions.

But Tom returned to the bedroom and he reached out to me. And he did it even though he knew that I had had cancer. We lay there in his bed, on blue sheets under a woven blanket, and talked. We talked about diseases, of all things. We talked about our earliest impressions of each other.

We spent four hours exchanging stories. While we talked there were moments of touching and stroking and the mapping of the face and body through our clothes. I basked in it, in Tom's fascination, his responsiveness to whatever I managed to give back. My tendency was to lie there and absorb it all and to say and do nothing. But sometimes I would let myself express something—by running my nails down his back or by offering a series of humorous kisses on his cheeks and eyes.

I discovered that Tom was many people. He was the carefully spoken, almost pedantic academician I first encountered. He was the uncertain boy grappling with my difficult news about cancer. And now he was a marvelously Elizabethan, ribald character. His appreciation of me seemed just a small part of his love of all women. He made me feel part of a bowl of beautiful ripe fruit to be appreciated by looking and touching and probably, someday, tasting.

I opened up in the luxury and comfort of that morning. But I admitted to Tom that I was afraid I would never be a sexy woman again.

"You are still very sexy," he said. "When I first saw you, I responded the same way as I guess other men probably do. I thought you were sexy not because you seemed to have big breasts, but because you have this laconic manner and lidded eyes."

So one by one I carefully exposed my fears, inviting Tom to reassure me. At one point, Tom tried to touch the outside of my shirt to test how the implant, the reconstructed breast, felt. I thought it was a gentle and sweet gesture. But I was incapable of anything overtly sexual. If I seemed aggressive, I was also shy. I wanted to test my powers on him, but I did not want to know the full extent of his powers on me. "Let's get up," I finally said, when it seemed like I had explored enough.

"Well, at least you know that you can still give a man a hard-on," he answered by way of reassurance and probably by way of protest. The fact is that that was all I really wanted to know for the moment.

After breakfast Tom walked me to my car. He brought with him the Indian shirt I had slept in. "Here, keep it. A memento of the first time you told," he said.

There are probably only three general responses that a woman can expect to receive—negative, positive, and neutral. The negative is what every woman fears most. But as my friends were so fond of telling me, "If that happens, then the guy's a jerk and just forget about him." But as much as I wanted to believe that, I couldn't ignore the physical realities.

Tom later told me that he feared his response. "I imagined my worst possible reaction, one where I said, 'This is horrible, this is awful, I can't look at this terrible disfigurement. I can't deal with it.' But I didn't want you to disappear either. I already knew I was interested in you. But a lot of it was ego, whether I could handle it or not."

So from Tom's perspective, news of my mastectomy was first

and foremost a personal test for him. Such an egocentric reaction was infuriating in a way, but it made perfect emotional sense. I was equally self-absorbed when I started dating Tom. And as it turned out, telling was a test for both of us—a shared experience in which we each felt somehow measured by my mastectomy.

Tom, of course, isn't every man. Some men show no reaction. Some openly admit to their "curiosity." I know because in the years since my mastectomy I have dated a number of men.

A few years after meeting Tom, I told a fellow named Roland as we sat overlooking the Golden Gate Bridge.

Roland was a journalist. I liked him but I didn't know why I liked him. Maybe we were too much alike, both sharp-minded and sharp-tongued and self-protective, engaged in an endless round of verbal repartee. It made us both a little defensive even though we understood each other perfectly.

It was our third date, and sitting there looking out over the water, I sensed that something was going to happen. First Roland and I wrestled, and when that didn't work out, we talked. We talked in the brutal, direct way that with the least bit of encouragement came naturally to both of us.

"I've had breast cancer. I had my breast removed," I threw out, assuming he'd figured it out during our brief wrestling match.

"No kidding? Let me see."

"No."

"Come on, I'm curious."

Roland said nothing except "I'm curious," and suddenly I wasn't feeling so tough or so forgiving. There was no sympathy, shock, or concern; no acknowledgment of the severity or the seriousness of what I had just revealed.

Who was to blame? I was at least partly responsible, because

I had announced the news like one of those barkers on the boardwalk at Coney Island.

I mention this encounter because how one tells has an impact on the man's response. My feigned toughness after some years of experience was matched by Roland's indifferent macho bluster.

But what about a neutral response? I believe it is absolutely reasonable to assume that a man might react neutrally to the news of cancer and a mastectomy. He might need more time to examine his feelings. But I also cannot deny what anyone who has ever experienced waiting for a never-to-be-received telephone call knows. Neutrality can be a silent way of bowing out. A post-mastectomy woman needs to remember this. Because the absence of a definite response is the sort of silence that inspires self-blame. It dredges up all the self-punishing reasons why a "neutral" man has imperceptibly faded away, even though it is mostly a statement about the man.

Whatever the reaction, I cannot deny that telling is an awful moment when it happens for the first time. There follows a tidal wave of fear and insecurity. Ironically, this was brought home to me even more when I was dating a doctor.

Although we hardly knew each other, I was unable to resist when a natural opportunity arose to announce my cancer and mastectomy to David. I had jokingly said something rude and nasty about doctors, and in self-defense David said, "Well, just wait till you really need one. What if you had cancer?"

I thought I was comfortable and secure enough to be fluid in my response about where and when to tell. And since he was a doctor, I thought it would be easy for him as well as for me.

"I have had cancer."

"What? Where?"

"Breast."

"What did you do?"

"Mastectomy."

"Any adjuvant?"

"No."

"Well, I'm sorry," he said. "You're young," switching suddenly from the purely clinical. And after his initial cross-examination, David was warm and gentle in his questions and comments, healing in his finely developed bedside manner.

I imagined that it was all very simple for him because he had seen mastectomies before—and I was giving a piece of medical history to a professional. But since I revealed it so early on, my insecurities rose up and I couldn't help but wonder why someone who dealt with illness and death and cancer all day long would want to unwind with more of the same at night.

Later on in our relationship, I was able to fill in the missing piece of the puzzle. I asked David what his private reaction had been.

"I was shocked."

I was shocked that he was shocked. "What do you mean? Why should a doctor be shocked at something like this?" I asked, getting angry.

"I'm a physician, but this was personal. So lots of things went through my mind. My overriding reaction was 'Oh my God,' because I already knew I liked you. But as a doctor who cares for a lot of cancer patients, I had to ask myself, 'Oh my God, am I going to get close to somebody in my personal life whom I might lose?' But I liked you, and that was reason enough to persist."

It was just as it had been with Tom. I had to stand up and

face the possibility that someone I liked might be unable to deal with the news of my breast cancer, even as I was still struggling to accept it myself. To this day, the stigma of cancer still looms largest at precisely the moment that I am about to tell.

7

The hardest thing about making love for a post-mastectomy woman is figuring out how to begin.

I mentioned my fears to Laura, an old friend from graduate school.

"Cover it up," she said, in her droll, matter-of-fact voice.

It was a brilliant and simple idea. Marriage and the comfortable life had added fifteen pounds to Laura's slender frame. So she resorted to camouflage.

"I always wear a silky camisole to bed," she told me. "Why should your situation be any different?"

It was a revelation to me. I suddenly realized that there were probably a lot of women out there who were worried about their bodies because of stomachs or thighs or cellulite. I wasn't alone. I tried to look at my mastectomy in a new light, a problem that might safely be grouped with all the other common female concerns. I was ecstatic to rejoin the rank and file of millions of benignly imperfect women.

"What've you got for a fake breast with no nipple?" I felt like asking at the lingerie counter when I began to hunt. (I was still in that long waiting period between breast reconstruction and the addition of a nipple, so my breast could settle.) And I was looking for something to provide the psychological illusion that nothing had changed at all. In order to imagine myself standing before Tom, I had to feel like the same woman, the same desirable woman I had known myself to be. And the camisole would provide a link with my sense of self from the past. But ironically, while the idea of a camisole gave me the personal security to push on, the process of actually obtaining it forced me to confront the painful fact of the radical change in myself.

I entered a tiny private dressing room with my collection of camisoles and bras in lace, silk, and satin. I pulled the curtain closed behind me with the care of a bank guard locking up the vault at night. There was nothing between me and the shopping floor but this flimsy curtain on shower hooks, and the curtain did not go all the way to the edge.

Under the bright lights, in front of a three-sided mirror, I took in my first professionally lit and multireflected view of my imperfect and still bright red scarred breasts. Then I pulled on a salmon-colored silk nightgown with spaghetti straps. The first thing I noticed was the difference in projection of my two breasts, and then the bony rib cage where there had once been soft and rounded flesh. I bent over and asked myself if the view was satisfactorily obscured. I was shy about revealing too much of myself because of the upsetting reality of an uneven cleavage and of one flowing breast and one shortened mound.

And I tried to envision how the garment would work in bed. Because when the time came, I wanted the coverup to suggest the kinds of seeing or touching I encouraged or discouraged and exactly where. Dismayed by the first nightgown, I took it off and pulled on another. I went through them one by one.

I went out again and scanned the merchandise in quiet desperation. I carried a second pile of garments into the dressing room and started over, stripping again and again in front of the mirror.

From behind me through the curtain came the voice of a man who wanted to buy a present. His very mission—a gift for a lover or a wife—stung. I kept my naked back to the curtain, lest he somehow glimpse me through the crack at its edge. I worried too that the saleswoman might barge in at any moment and that he would catch a glimpse of me then. Long after there was silence, I continued to cringe. I realized I didn't want the saleswoman to see me either.

I was still trying things on an hour later. I had started crying after twenty minutes. But finally I found a sword and shield: a silk camisole. Its line covered my scars. Its turquoise color brightened my face. The overall effect was good enough to plug the dam against my still-oncoming tears.

Then, on the brink of merely entertaining the idea of sleeping with a man, I suffered another post-mastectomy emotional crisis. I realized that clothing doesn't simply conceal. It is designed to *enhance* and even *emphasize* exactly the things I had wanted it to hide. Yet I could see the irony. I had always presented myself nude when I first slept with someone. But here I was, on the brink of a new intimacy, and I was out shopping for a veil.

But what else could I do? I felt Tom and I might soon make love, and I could conceive of no other protection against that oncoming crisis than to purchase emotional insurance in the form of a 100 percent silk coverup.

I believed that the sight of my bare breasts would upset Tom. But I feared his reaction mostly because I was so unsure of my own. My new breast looked to me like the contour on a window dummy and felt almost as hard. I was ambivalent about it except for the fact that it was attached to my body; it was a part of me.

The coverup I bought was an early and necessary transitional tool for me. It seemed to allow me to take that risk to move on. It was a guise, a way to focus less on my surgery, be more of myself and, hopefully, let the sex drive take over on the still unspecified occasion of my first sexual encounter.

I took home my small purchase and the still-burning visual imprint of my ravaged body as seen from three different angles under bright lights. I went home to worry about sex, still bitter that I had been harshly redefined. And I did worry. I resolved to make sure the encounter took place at my home. I thought it would make me feel more comfortable and more in control of the details. Never mind the camisole. I also worried about the quality of the light. Only a very narrow range—namely, pitch black—would do. But maybe in time, low lighting, candlelight, mood lighting, even fish-tank-illuminated rooms would become acceptable.

The idea of actual intercourse brought up more fears. I wasn't so much concerned about the physical comfort of different positions as the psychological comfort. Because even with the emotional protection of my camisole, I found myself working out that, if I was lying on my back, the mastectomy would seem less obtrusive. I could easily imagine how, with me on top, I would feel that my breasts were on display. And that was my big fear. This, then, was the result of my shopping spree. A lift for my spirits? No. What I brought home was mostly ruminations and pain.

I no longer took my physical desirability for granted. Despite all my planning, I wasn't ready to handle an abrupt confrontation with my breasts as I had experienced it by myself in the dressing room that afternoon. But I did not regard my fear and anxiety as things to try to avoid or escape. I saw them as warning signals.

In my case, the anxiety was about exposure, the exposure of taking off all my clothes. Probably not an unusual thought for a post-mastectomy woman. And like the early process of forgetting about cancer and mastectomy for first a minute and then a day, I knew that this process would also be a slow one to unfold.

I had bought a coverup to quell my anxiety. But even at the beginning I was aware that if hiding behind a coverup became a permanent feature of my behavior, it would become a barrier to healing if not a serious emotional impasse. And I have no doubt that every woman hiding behind a coverup knows why she is there and whether it has become a cloak for depression and despair or a way to deny the constant visual reminder of an illness that seems to have changed her life forever. I believe the failure to show, like the failure to tell, when it goes on too long, promotes pain rather than intimacy in women's lives.

What does it mean, then, when the covering up is finally over? Is it the end of bad feelings, a rejection of an assumed repulsiveness? Is it the opportunity to touch the scar and love it, even in erotic situations? I believe that the answer is yes.

8

During the weeks leading up to my night of anticipated lovemaking with Tom, I tried on my new coverup daily before the mirror. I rehearsed with it. What happened when the right strap fell down? Or the left? What if both straps fell down? I tested each hypothesis over and over until I felt satisfied that my scars wouldn't be exposed.

On Saturday, I had my cervical cap installed by four in the afternoon. I felt my nerve endings—at least those that remained—reawaken with a surge. I was hell-bent on the *idea* of making love. The actuality, however, despite all my preparations, was another matter. My mind thought it a good idea, but my emotions conspired in another direction.

Tom arrived at five-thirty, and like a stereotypical California couple we drank wine, ate smoked oysters, and talked. At sunset, we went for a walk on the beach and talked more. We walked separately for a good part of the way, but from time to time Tom put his arm around me, and eventually, as a courtesy, I wrapped my arm around him. And yet it didn't feel quite right. That old tension, present on our first couple of dates, was back. Then I had blamed it on the need to tell. But now Tom knew about the mastectomy.

When the sun set, we left the beach to get dinner. And sure enough, we were unable to agree on a restaurant. I insisted on adhering to my new non-meat diet, a change I had made to promote good health. But I felt foolish, since now it was making eating out so difficult. The whole issue of what to eat was another reminder of cancer. And this was the night that I wanted to put it all behind me.

"Don't feel hopeless. Don't give up even if everything goes wrong," I reasoned with myself. I felt as I had in the third grade when I got so wound up in anticipation of my big birthday party that I cried.

As it turned out, the restaurant was perfect. It was a pizza parlor, an old-style place with very low light and a lot of dusty plastic grape clusters and wine bottles hung from a lattice ceiling. It was popular with the college set. And I was more than aware of feeling exactly their age. Tom ordered a large carafe of wine and I knew it would be a long, leisurely dinner. I started to relax.

We talked for hours. I told Tom more about my past, about my experiences in graduate school, about my family, and about my relationships with Ari, Brian, Uwe, and Bill. What I especially noticed as Tom listened and responded was a softness, an almost feminine side. I hoped that that quality would make him a rare and compassionate lover. Then Tom talked to me about women in his past, and of his feelings of magnetic attraction to what usually turned out to be Jewish women. He was also excited by the beautiful and exotic mix of women on the West Coast. "Even in Daly City there is a flood of exquisite Asian girls from the high schools at three in the afternoon," he said. "How can anyone call Daly City an ugly place?"

I laughed. My God, was he really hanging around school yards in Daly City just to admire the girls? He has a broad appreciation of women, I thought. But a part of me was immediately distressed. There was no comparison between me and those blossoming young creatures carrying their schoolbooks. I didn't know what to make of Tom and his innocently expressed fantasies.

He couldn't have known it, but his passing observations fueled my self-rejection and, by extension, my self-protective rejection of him. I quickly misinterpreted his remarks, taking each one as a slight. I mean, if those Asian high school girls were so important and so lovely, why was he bothering with me? I decided that if he wanted them he could have them. I withdrew, hurt and defensive.

I couldn't help noticing that he made no effort to touch me, to hold hands across the table. There was no pressure of knee upon knee. I felt no desire for it, yet I missed it. And I backed deeper into my hole. Tom kept talking and I nodded, brooding over my self-punishing thoughts. I could see the great distance looming between us, despite our physical proximity. I made one mighty last-ditch effort to save myself and the evening.

"I'm so fearful still," I blurted out, "I'm not acting like I usually do. I'm a flirt. But I'm avoiding all of this with you. There doesn't seem to be any of that magnetism you keep talking about." I wanted to know what Tom was feeling because in truth I couldn't feel a thing.

"Don't worry, I'm in no hurry," he said.

He seemed to be telling me that he didn't want to rush me into a physical relationship. How ironic. My cervical cap had already been installed for eight hours. Tom assured me that he felt electricity between us and reached for my hand. We made contact. But for my part, I still couldn't feel those electrons flow.

Back at my apartment after dinner, we sat at opposite ends of the brown velvet couch for at least half an hour. I made what felt like the very bold move of rearranging my body so that I could snuggle against his chest. In a few minutes we were kissing.

A good idea, but I felt as if I had forgotten how. Uncertain, I wanted to stop. But it was Tom who finally pulled back.

"There's a bus back over the bridge at one-thirty A.M.," he said. "Am I supposed to be on it?" I didn't answer. I wanted him to stay but I couldn't openly admit it.

"Would you like to stretch out on my bed?" I asked, ten minutes after I knew his bus had left.

"There are other buses," Tom said. "Are you sure you want me to stay?"

"I'm inviting you," I admitted at long last. And then it dawned on me. It wasn't clear which one of us was more afraid.

I opened my futon and arranged the covers and pillows. Then I went into the bathroom and put on my new silk camisole. Tom was waiting for me when I came out.

I turned off the light. I didn't look to see if Tom was watching me. A part of me hoped that he was, but I was too shy to make certain. The camisole looked nice I thought, even sexy. But I couldn't pretend that it was just a ploy. It was a psychological necessity.

I hesitated. Which side of the bed should I take? I chose the left side because then, when on my side face-to-face with

Tom, my reconstructed right breast would be covered and hidden by the angle of my body and my arm against the bed. I wanted my natural breast to be the accessible one; I wanted to feel it against his body.

The stereo was on and the dim light from its dial spread over my bed, lighting the room in the way that the little lights on the sides of seats in movie theaters illuminate the aisles. Just enough so you don't fall down. I had always considered seeing my partner essential. But now I was more concerned about not being seen. I wanted to hide in the darkness, but not just to remove the sight of my scarred breast or my fake one. I wanted to hide completely—my reactions, my facial expressions, whatever I was doing, thinking, or feeling. I turned off the stereo. And in the darkness I felt essentially alone.

It was so dark that I could barely make out Tom's silhouette. But he was there to feel and touch. And for a while, it was the same old awkwardness. We were like any two people who lie down together for the first time. There were the usual bumps and mistakes and attempts to figure out what the other was feeling or wanting. We were like two clumsy dance partners, not knowing who should take the lead. I sensed that it was meant to be me. But I was vague and unhelpful. In the first moments, I wanted only the pleasure of being closely held and I luxuriated in a feeling of well-being.

But I soon began to fret. Even in the darkness, I wanted to know the camisole's precise location on my body. Was it covering my scars and the implant? My concern for the visual was irrational yet persistent. And it subsided only slightly as I noticed that the preliminary steps to lovemaking had not come to any abrupt halt.

The camisole was doing its job, perpetuating the illusion of uniformity and symmetry in my own mind. And so it was that I was able to lean over Tom and let him reach his hands up and hold both my breasts. I liked that. I liked the illusion of the perfect symmetry of my two breasts and the momentary experience that what was there under the camisole was not one real and one fake, but all me.

But I shuddered when Tom exposed my natural breast. I imagined that he could see the scars in the darkness and I held my breath. But Tom seemed not to notice what I was sure he could see. Maybe the scars aren't visible, I conceded. But I knew they could be felt. And from that point forward, every touch was bittersweet.

Fortunately, my natural breast retained its sensitivity. But that very sensitivity sent back messages of the thickened seams traversing my breast. Each touch sent a heat image to my brain, an image that became a photograph of the battered terrain. I began mourning my breasts in practice. I missed not only my absent right breast, I missed my left breast as well. It was intact, but altered. With my natural breast exposed I experienced for the first time what it meant to have it reduced. So this is what I've got, I lamented. I've got a pert, pointy, scarred, and oddly smaller version of myself on the left and something that totally lacks sensation, basically an updated version of a wooden leg, on the right. So why the hell focus here? I communicated my unspoken directions to Tom.

The other aspects of lovemaking intensified and, as they did, my natural expectation for sensations did too. To my surprise, the camisole had already become too much of a good thing. I was willing to expose most of my torso if only I could find a way to do it without stripping completely. I was willing to let my natural breast be exposed, fondled, and handled. But I would never let the camisole slip from the reconstructed half of my body. I tried to move it up so I could feel my stomach against him, but silk is slippery and it wouldn't stay. So, in order to hide my breast and preserve my self-image, I ended up having to cover some of the good things that had survived.

If there was any climax on my part to this first sexual encounter with Tom, it was that self-congratulatory instant when I had actually done it. If there was any involvement, it was only with myself. My primary goal had been to sleep with a "stranger," a new man, after mastectomy, and now I had. And after it was all over, I felt lonely.

Afterward, I confessed my feelings to Tom. "Don't," he said. "I am here and I will be here in the morning."

Only the next morning did I understand his cryptic assurance of the night before. He was there to make love to me again. I was pleased, but much more than pleased I was frightened. My room was filled with light! There was no possibility of hiding. I hadn't planned for this. Were the implant and scars hidden? But with the camisole still on, Tom uncovered my natural breast. Oh God, I said to myself. I kept my eyes closed but I seemed to see the scars in the daylight. I protested, as if to ask, "Do you know what you're doing wanting to kiss that thing, my breast? It's been cut up." But he seemed more intent on the kissing than on my concerns. And with his attentions, the scars actually faded from red to pink where I saw them behind my still tightly closed eyes.

I could start to feel my emotions welling up. I listened to what Tom had to say. I accepted his murmured compliments. I even allowed the possibility that I might someday like my body again.

Still, I wanted to take Tom back in time and show him old photographs and say, "See here. This was me before and you would have loved my breasts." It was as if there had been a death and now there was only memory.

Naturally, Tom was also seeking assurances, and I tried to reciprocate. I told him that I liked his nose. Talk about reserve. And I also intimated that I liked penises. Tom began to question me directly about my preferences—what he did or didn't do, what he should or shouldn't do. I thought then of all the silenced desires, all the untried experiments, all the self-imposed limits.

In a few short sentences I detailed the whole list of what I knew I liked, more than I had ever admitted to anyone. There was a new kind of openness between us, and something to feel very good about. I decided to let go.

Ever since Dr. Elliot's first pronouncement about mastectomy, I had assumed that the act of making love would be the big hurdle I would have to cross. And until I crossed it, with Tom, it was. Then I fell fairly comfortably into an active sex life.

Yet I woke up one Saturday morning about a month later and did not want to move. It was foggy and I lay in bed in a state of dark defiance. Tom was due to arrive, and I wasn't looking forward to it. After only a few short weeks of making love, the glow had already worn off. I didn't feel like seeing him, didn't want to contend with his company, didn't want to plan what we would do.

I had been feeling this way for days, and it was surprising—even to me. But then I realized that the root of all these emotions was one simple fact: Tom had never seen me naked. I was afraid that when the time came to make love nude, Tom was going to reject me.

I had expected sex to be the great hurdle. But no, there was a new risk to run, physically and psychologically. That was the source of my hostility, my feelings of pressure and resentment, ambivalence and tension. I was backing away in anticipation of having to expose my body, I realized, trying to escape and avoid my sense of loss before it became a certainty. I understood then that the process of my self-acceptance was not over. Because even though Tom called me regularly and was interested in seeing me again and again, I thought I would lose him.

I was afraid to test him. What if he couldn't handle it? Would I have the strength to try again with someone else, and where on earth would that someone come from? It was as though I had lost track of the natural course of events—the mysterious ways in which relationships progress, unfold, and change.

My questions and fears were natural. I still persisted in covering up, feeling self-conscious because one nipple was gone, because sensation was gone in my reconstructed breast. I still recoiled whenever Tom attempted to nuzzle anywhere near my breasts. At the moment when we first made love, I thought the issue of sex and mastectomy was resolved. But now I realized I still had a long way to go.

When Tom arrived at my house, we decided to drive through all the hidden, usually unseen, sometimes depressed neighborhoods of San Francisco: Bay View, Visitación Valley, Crocker-Amazon, McLaren Park, and then on to Stern Grove. Stern Grove almost always sits in fog but miraculously on this day it was warm and sunny. It seemed that everyone else in San Francisco expected to find fog, as Tom and I were alone in this public park except for an occasional dog. We walked through a grove of eucalyptus trees and across a meadow, and around a small lake hidden by pampas grass. We stopped and, hidden from view, we kissed. I remember thinking how nice it was to be part of the couple kissing instead of an observer, even if there was no one there to watch us.

We sat down on the grass. It was silent except for the birds, and my attention focused on Tom's voice as I lay in the sun with my eyes closed. Then I interrupted him. "How are you holding up?" Tom understood my question immediately.

"In a way it's like I haven't had to deal with it yet," he said. "I'm getting to know you better, but I've shunted both the illness and the mastectomy out of my mind—especially since I haven't really seen how you look."

"What do you mean?"

"At first, when you explained that you weren't ready for me to see you, I understood that. Actually I thought maybe it was just as well because I wasn't sure if I was ready to look. I thought the camisole was a good idea. It was kind of sexy. And you know I'm attracted and excited by you. And by concealing that part of you, you've forced me to focus elsewhere."

"Is there anything wrong with that?"

"No. Nothing. It has been entirely pleasing. But you know, now I'm curious, though a little scared. I know that your body has been altered in some severe way. I'd be lying if I didn't say that there is something upsetting and powerful about it. I keep pretending that, as a lover, you have an odd quirk that demands that you leave some bit of clothing on. But it leaves me with this nagging feeling that I haven't dealt with anything yet. I'm full of fervor and worry. And," he added, "it's up to you, how we take things step by step."

I listened attentively to what was between the lines. Tom gave no hint that he would look at me and say, "No, I can't deal with this," and then walk away forever. I was encouraged by what he told me. He cared for me and had obviously wondered about what was appropriate and what should happen next. It all seemed to hinge on me and on his "seeing"—whenever it was that I decided to let him.

"I realized only this morning that I still haven't revealed my whole body to you. I was shocked and scared when it finally hit me," I told him. I was talking about trust—my willingness to give over a very wounded part of myself and my belief in Tom's ability to offer the proper response. Our discussion was evidence of my growing self-confidence, but I still felt in constant danger of complete collapse.

That night I sat on the same old couch in the living room as though we had never made love before. I was waiting until it was absolutely necessary to go into the bedroom, waiting until we were both completely exhausted. And even then, the moment I stood in the lamplight next to the bed, I faltered. I got only as far as taking my slacks off and then fell on the bed in the rest of my clothes. Here I am again, I thought, coyness herself. I was still wary, skirting the boundaries of emotional rather than physical pain. Was I too ugly and lopsided to go through with it?

It was obvious to me that it was time to make love nude. But in my heightened state of expectation and anxiety, I was unable to make it happen all alone. I wanted to be taken by surprise, to be coaxed and seduced; I didn't want to participate, to make decisions.

Tom came into the bedroom and put his arms around me. He began kissing me and I felt instantly uncomfortable. I tried to ignore my discomfort, but there was no way. No matter what Tom did, I was distracted by wondering, Will I really let him take all my clothes off? Finally, he just looked at me and said, "Undress."

"What a great rear you have," he told me when I was only partially nude, offering me encouragement to go on. And then in the half light of the room, Tom looked at me naked for the first time.

He waited a moment and finally mumbled something along the lines of "It's not that bad." In the past it seemed as if I had always heard "Oh, you have fantastic breasts." Now, on the first occasion of exposing my breasts to Tom, I heard only lukewarm words of consolation. But before I could react, Tom did. He was suddenly caught up in a wave of sympathy for me. He squeezed me violently and whispered, "Oh, you poor darling." And that was too much for me. With his words my own feelings exploded, feelings I had not allowed myself just minutes, not to mention months, before.

I was not just crying, but wailing from a place deep inside my soul, some unmapped region I had been to only once before—when I thought my life might shortly end. Tom's sympathy confirmed that something awful had been done to me, and my own pain welled up in waves of emotion. And I was shocked by my own response. It was as if I were at my own funeral and suddenly sat up to scream and cry with the assembled mourners.

"Don't feel bad," Tom said as I cried.

"No, no," I answered. "You don't understand. In some ways I feel better, much better, it's a relief. After all, it's over with now." The burden, the source of the tremendous tension and anxiety, was gone.

"I feel better," I said, still crying, and it was true.

"Good, good. I'm glad to hear it," Tom said. "I thought you were crying because you felt so sad."

"I do feel sad," I answered. And the unveiling was the crux of it all. I was naked and exposed.

As if to comfort me, Tom told me about his own sexual fears. I was touched by his gentle attempts to first soothe me and then continue his sexual advances. He began to kiss and touch both my breasts in an effort to make up for the pain. But I felt nothing. I was too naked, too exposed. I was raw from crying. Tom faded into sleep. I just lay there quietly, emotionally exhausted. I had the odd feeling that I didn't want to miss anything. Finally, I realized it was simply Tom's company that I would miss when I fell asleep.

If I was nude, exposed, and emotionally open at the instant when I fell asleep, I was anxious again when I opened my eyes. I was immediately uncomfortable in the light, even though I was under the covers. Tom went into the kitchen to make coffee and I used the opportunity to fly into the bathroom. And just like the time when I told Tom about my cancer and mastectomy, I was afraid to come out. I got as far as putting my hand on the doorknob and then I hesitated and froze. I knew Tom would be looking at me from the bed, watching me walk toward him. I could not propel myself, nude, into the line of his gaze. It was like a panic at great heights or like walking over a bridge when you can see water below through the grating. My solution was to pull my turquoise camisole from the closet, slip it on, and only then trot out.

"Oh," Tom said.

"I couldn't get out of the bathroom without putting something on. I just couldn't," I said, and threw myself in his arms.

"Oh, so you've regressed some, is that it?" he teased.

But even if Tom didn't mind, I did. It seemed as if I was still fighting with myself and, consequently, fighting Tom. And the battle, though virtually silent, was taking its toll. I had always been preoccupied with the man's response, and what

I found was that I was the one who could not respond. My mind and emotions were elsewhere. I was worrying over how to hide my nudity in daylight from a man who was trying to be my lover.

I simply could not imagine myself as the object of Tom's attention. Why would he want to make love to me now—nude— in the brightness of morning? But Tom was trying to do just that. He was trying to seduce me and I was busy cataloging my imperfections—one by one—to myself. Yet during my self-conscious inventory taking, I finally accepted that I was rejecting him even as I worried over being rejected.

So I just pulled off the camisole. It was a pure act of will, a conscious decision to plunge forward and regain the ground I had lost.

I would let Tom look at me in a studied, calm, even clinical way. I wanted to break down the barriers of self-consciousness and curiosity and move on to familiarity. So he looked at me and I looked at him looking at me. And there was something about this moment that was exactly as it should be, an objective staring down by the two of us at this strange part of me—my chest. I hoped it would make life easier.

I asked Tom what he thought. "It's not the imperfections," he said. "But I see the image of a knife cutting through that area. It doesn't repulse me. It's just that I feel sympathy for the process and for you."

That day we made love several times. I responded to his advances and even silently offered my fake breast. I put aside my own fears and feelings of repulsion and admitted that this was all that I had to offer. I knew it was up to me to let Tom know what I wanted. He needed directions, that he should do this or that to my breasts, so that he didn't feel that he was forcing attention onto them. In fact, Tom asked me many times if my remaining breast was still sensitive and if I wanted to be touched there and I said yes several times. Certainly my breast got as much attention as I wanted. But I'm not sure it got as much attention as Tom had to give. Still, my emerging feelings about my breasts were something new. I had decided to stop apologizing for them.

Before Tom left the next morning, he began taking pictures of me in my robe. I was sitting out on my fire escape suspended over a garden and looking back into the living room through the frame of the window. Tom had taken pictures of me once before weeks earlier, and I would not sit still. But this time Tom's picture taking became an expression of his sense of my beauty. I found out, unexpectedly and unconsciously, that I was beautiful to Tom at just the moment when I was feeling the least attractive of all. So I not only let him photograph me, I let him direct me like a model. It was a sign of increased trust, an extension of the healing of the night before. And it was a gesture of appreciation on my part. I was pleased that Tom wanted to record this important morning on film.

I can't help thinking of what other women have since shared with me. A married woman of fifty-five once confided to me that it took her five years to let her husband look at her again. Another woman I talked to, who was single and thirty-eight, reacted at the opposite extreme. She seemed to use sex as a way of denying her cancer, as an affirmation of life. But, as she acknowledged, it was an act of desperation.

Of course, sleeping with Tom and being nude in front of him for that first time didn't mean that I had fully adjusted to mastectomy. These were at best healthy statements of intent. They were evidence that I continued to subscribe to the idea of a satisfying sexual life. But despite my belief that I wasn't "any less of a woman," there were many moments when I didn't feel convinced. It was time and risk-taking that finally completed the process—to the extent that it is ever totally complete.

Because like almost every woman, I felt awkward with sexual openness after mastectomy. And I know that there are still countless women who in many different ways let fear and shame take precedence over their need for what an intimate relationship provides. Single women in particular ask themselves why a man would want to adjust when there are scores of two-breasted women to choose from. But what motivates a man is always an underlying interest in the woman. No matter how old or how new the relationship, a man rarely reduces the sum total of a woman to the sum total of her breasts. Like me, it is usually the woman, still picking the jagged pieces of her self-image and self-esteem up off the floor, who's doing the counting.

It was the fear of loss of control that held me back; experiencing the shame of cancer in a sexual context was not unlike cancer's first early terror. Post-mastectomy sex is exposure at the deepest level of a woman's experience, a naked confrontation with her vulnerability. It concentrates the full force of the days, weeks, months, or years of physical and emotional pain from cancer into a single moment. The experience is so sharp as to make some women imagine that it is impossible to face. I cannot minimize the pain of such exposure, but I do believe that despite all the emotional barriers to sex and nudity, avoiding them is harder still.

9

There is nothing to do about all these concerns but live through them. Fortunately, in the years since my mastectomy, avenues of information and support for the women who must live through such concerns have opened up. There is an increased focus within the medical and psychiatric literature about the impact of cancer on sexuality, and health professionals are better prepared to talk about and deal with the psychosocial aspects of cancer, including sex. I remember that three or four years ago, when I first sought a mastectomy support group relevant to me in San Francisco, I found what I considered a coffee klatch instead. But there are now three groups in this city that feature sexuality among their issues of interest and concern. In addition, there are individual psychotherapists specializing in breast-cancer counseling, and there are support groups geared specifically to younger and often single women. These deal not only with sexuality, but with the loss of fertility, since in the years since my own diagnosis, chemotherapy almost routinely follows surgery in the treatment of premenopausal women. This local trend in support groups has been repeating itself nationally.

As a long-time volunteer with Reach to Recovery, I have witnessed how addressing sexual concerns has become a part of the training of volunteers. Because it is an unfortunate fact that a woman with breast cancer cannot avoid much of what I have described. Women talking to women is as it should be, since those most often charged with her medical care have no practical way to understand what a woman faces. Regardless of their gender, they work with the hard-edged and clinical details of prognosis and choices for treatment and that's all. But since a care giver's role is both to make recommendations for treatment and to offer support, it is time to formalize ways in which the information exchange starts to move from patient to doctor. I offer this book not only to other post-mastectomy women, but to medical professionals as well.

On a more personal note, these days I listen to Tom's travails and woes about other women, and occasionally, when emotions run high, he has taken me by the shoulders and looked me in the eyes and said, "Anyway, it's you that I love." If you wonder if I've said, "Okay, let's get married," I haven't. There is a hard edge to my personality that I fear would overrun Tom if it was given half a chance. The qualities in Tom that made him an excellent first lover after my mastectomy—what I call his softness—were in fact some of the same ones that probably ended our romantic relationship. I began to link Tom's uncertainty about the direction of his life, at the time, his doubts and insecurities or how he handled adversity, with that "softness." It reminded me of my father and what I regard as the tragedy of my father's life and death. I saw my father's inaction give rise to disappointment and frustration at home, so seeing it in Tom frightened me. It was a time in my life when I was struggling with my own sense of self and my own place in the world and I found that I still didn't have the emotional resources to support Tom in his struggles. After nine months, the romantic aspect of our relationship ended.

Yet, we have remained close. I think that no matter what's been cut off or what else gets cut off or whoever else comes along, Tom and I are always going to be friends. We speak almost weekly and see each other often, and I feel that with this small margin of distance between us, I am better able to be a good and supportive friend to him.

I discussed the end of our romantic relationship with my therapist, Sam. "How do you feel about your body, since you may soon be going back out into the world?"

I could hear the emotion in my voice, but what I said to Sam surprised even me. "My breast won't be a factor. Whoever is next will accept it."

Sam seemed startled by my confidence. For the most part, I owed this leap to Tom. And so far, my prediction has proved correct.

While I can talk about cancer and mastectomy with more ease these days, there is still the moment when it comes time to go to bed with a new man. And I approach it as I did with Tom. Almost four years later and I'm still wearing that turquoise camisole my first time out. Only it is no longer a matter of shame. It's ironic, I suppose, that I can trust a man enough to sleep with him, but that it takes sleeping with him to trust him enough to finally undress. So for me, nudity is still the moment of truth.

What is different is that it is no longer such a dramatic process. I am willing to take my camisole off by the second encounter. I go to bed with it on and take it off in the course of lovemaking because, as I have said before, the damn thing gets in the way. By morning, I am willing to get up and shower, and soon after that, simply walk around in the nude. I have truly come to know and accept that the success or failure of any relationship is really a reflection of the two personalities involved and not a reflection of one or the other of the two bodies.

I can see that my mastectomy was in some ways a convenient metaphor for something much deeper that was missing in myself. Probably well before I had the mastectomy, I had rejected a part of myself, and as the truism goes, I could not fully accept another person until I had accepted myself. While I couched my feelings at the time in questions of whether or not Tom or some other man was the right, perfect man for me, I knew that by merely asking such a loaded question the answer was going to have to be no.

Some women may feel driven to settle down after mastectomy, but I seemed to require the opposite. This is not surprising, since I was unable or unwilling to settle down even before the mastectomy. If I had ever imagined I wanted a deep love as soon as I could find it, I came to the clear realization that I did not.

My mastectomy was an obvious sign that something was missing. But after I proved to myself that it wasn't only my breast that was missing, I wanted to know what was. Cancer had ripped me open. The experience left me with the realization that it was time to put myself back together in a new way. Through my conversations with my therapist, I saw that what was required was a deep and fundamental internal change.

Nothing less would give positive meaning to my cancer experience or real hope to my future relationships. I began the long process of learning more about myself with Sam's help, and in the company of other men.

"There's still so much I want to know about what will happen in the world," Frank Oppenheimer told me, "but for you, there is still so much you want to know about yourself." That was shortly before Frank died of cancer at the age of seventy-three and shortly after I had found out that I had breast cancer. Frank was one of the few truly brilliant men I have known. He could see that my understanding of myself and my relationships were still at the stage of a child who writes in crude block-lettered print, aching to attain the rounded forms of script.

Learning has been a painfully slow process. It's as though I am grappling with the issue of desirability even now. But it is not my physical desirability any longer, so much as emotional. I am still struggling with true intimacy, that refinement of human interaction that I have somehow eluded or that has somehow eluded me. What is different, though, is that now I carry with me the benefits of what I have learned not only from Frank but from Tom and the other relationships that I have had over the past four years.

As for Uwe, we are just plain family. We argue, get angry, borrow money, confide, begrudgingly love each other, and talk about our other loves to each other. Part of what unites Uwe and me is our pain and our confusion in the face of intimacy and love. We're like two weeds fighting our way together, up toward the light. He left town for several months recently and we posed for a farewell picture. I thought it would be nice for me to have one while he was gone, with Uwe sitting down of course and me standing, our arms wrapped around each other and our heads tilted inward, near the top. Even though the picture was supposed to be for me, Uwe took it along with him and left me with only a Xerox copy. I was surprised that he wanted it, but more than surprised, I was touched. He is nothing more and nothing less than one of my hardest-to-figure but closest friends.

As far as my family is concerned, Marcia, the psychologist and the only true nurturer among us, has taken pains to get the family to be closer. Two years ago, she and I flew to New York at the same time and, quite by chance, managed to see almost all of my father's seven brothers and sisters and their families together, for the first time in fifteen years. And a new pattern within my immediate family has emerged. It started the year after both Marcia and I were diagnosed. Having finished law school, my sister Gale passed the bar exam at age forty-one and, as if that weren't enough, she also went out and got married. The wedding was a joyful occasion, celebrated outdoors in a garden in full bloom after a year of flowers given only in sadness and turmoil. My whole family gathered together in San Francisco for more than a month, with the wedding as the centerpiece of our extended visit. My mother and Sol arrived early, and this time even Sol got to stay in my apartment—breathing hard and complaining all the way to the top of Nob Hill and up three flights of steps to my door.

My mother, Sol, my two sisters and their families, and I now gather regularly for a month each summer. We rent one large house in which we all try to fit so that whether we are at Lake Tahoe or in Steamboat Springs, Colorado, or somewhere in Europe, we manage to re-create the same old crowded, teeming life of our childhood home. Naturally, that month each year brings up a lot. It has given me insight into both my hostility and my reserve within my family, how my role within it somehow evolved into giving little and observing a lot and no doubt judging too much. But it has also revealed the opposite: how my relationship with my family is stronger than any disappointment about what I may have wanted, rarely expressed, and therefore never gotten, and how our ties are deeper than whatever anger I may feel. There are moments when it's exactly as it was when we were growing up—competition, bickering, and arguing, but also eating, dancing, and laughter.

As for my own body, I returned to the hospital one more time, one and a half years after my mastectomy, to add a nipple and thereby complete my new breast. The skin for my nipple was taken from my groin area, and I told my doctor that if nothing else, I wanted all the hair follicles out. But the fact is that, even with a made-to-order surrogate nipple, I've gotten what women hate most, some hair. The nipple certainly completes my sense of symmetry, but like all the other parts of the reconstruction, it is human and therefore imperfect.

My reconstructed breast is still hard. The scar tissue surrounding it causes constriction and the breast still needs to be shoved around roughly once in a while. I try to do it myself, but it takes someone on the outside to do a really good job. It is usually a sure sign of my trust in a man when I invite him to massage my breast for me.

Since Tom there have been a number of men and I fully expect that there will be more until I get it absolutely right. But that will be sometime in the future. Because my story and this book do not end like a fairy tale. My idea of the perfect conclusion to a life's story has broadened since the days when I was six years old. That I have overcome the physical and emotional hardships of cancer and mastectomy is my perfect ending. It is a fitting resolution to my arduous struggle. And I know now that the satisfactions I seek come from within. A handsome man would be nice, but this was always, first and foremost, a story of self-acceptance.

I learned that mastectomy and cancer are not the problems in my life. I resolved the issues of self-image and self-esteem, but I have had to tackle some even deeper parts of myself.

When cancer shook me to the core, it loosened the bonds and layers of protection I have always kept locked around myself. Yet even my mastectomy and the fear of cancer did not totally change what I can only describe as my fear in the face of love. It has taken me four years to finally uncover my long-hidden and yet basic desires for intimacy. Simple as it seems, it is only now that I can say that I feel ready to love. I see now that all along the misapprehension has been my own. Most of the men I have known were willing in their own way to love me or at least to see beyond what I myself saw as the problem. But for me, they could be little more than milestones in my own development. Until now.

Just six months ago I met Colin. He's only a few years older than I am and, I think, we are both late bloomers. The first time we spoke, we talked until four-thirty in the morning, and sometime during that marathon conversation, I told him I had had a mastectomy and it was clear that my news made no difference. I was struck immediately by his directness and openness, which left so little room for doubt. For a woman like me, such frankness was disarming and forced me to respond in kind. I know I still have things to learn, but sometimes I wonder if Colin couldn't be the whole lesson.

It has been hard work, but now I can start to see the fruits of all my efforts—the blossoming of a true and long-lasting intimacy—and the sorts of feelings that have been made possible by the dramatic events of the past four years. Instead of focusing on cancer, survival, and sexuality—the concerns that a post-mastectomy woman deals with all together and all at once—I have finally made my way toward a new set of worries and concerns, the joyous and essential ones of life.